"They sat silently, staring at the wreckage. The Outcast had saved the worst till last."

DOUBLECROSS

MISSION ATOMIC

THE 39 CLUES

SARWAT CHADDA

SCHOLASTIC INC.

To the fans. May your lives be full of
AWESOMESAUCE!
–S.C.

Library of Congress Control Number: 2016934378

ISBN 978-0-545-76751-4

10 9 8 7 6 5 4 3 2 1   16 17 18 19 20/0

Cover, back cover and endpaper photos ©: atoms design: ihor_seamless/
Shutterstock, Inc.; equations: Marina Sun/Shutterstock, Inc.; nuclear tanks:
Freddie Bethune for Scholastic; blueprint: amgun/Shutterstock, Inc.

Interior photos ©: 2: Ken Karp for Scholastic; 56 background: CG Textures;
56 main: Ken Karp for Scholastic; 120: Dan Kosmayer/Shutterstock, Inc.;
125: Charice Silverman for Scholastic; 139: Ken Karp for Scholastic;
144–145: Charice Silverman for Scholastic; 209 bee: Alekss/Fotolia;
209 skull on bee: Charice Silverman for Scholastic.

First edition, July 2016

Printed in the U.S.A.   23

Scholastic US: 557 Broadway · New York, NY 10012
Scholastic Canada: 604 King Street West · Toronto, ON M5V 1E1
Scholastic New Zealand Limited: Private Bag 94407 · Greenmount, Manukau 2141
Scholastic UK Ltd.: Euston House · 24 Eversholt Street · London NW1 1DB

PROLOGUE

"Dan! Dan! Can you hear me?"

Dan gripped the cell phone, squeezing it so hard that the plastic creaked. "Amy! I'm here!"

He shook it. He could hardly see her: the screen was a blizzard of static, his sister's face a frightened mask.

Her voice crackled through the speakers. "I—I don't have much time, Dan. You have to listen. . . ."

"Where are you? Tell me!"

Amy sighed. Her shoulders slumped and she seemed to crumble from inside. He'd never seen her so small, so beaten.

How could she be? She was his sister. They'd been through everything together and had always come out on top.

Always.

"Amy, tell me."

Her face was stained with bruises.

Dan gritted his teeth. Whoever had done this to Amy would pay a thousand times over.

She put her fingertips against the camera of her own phone, as if she was trying to reach through the screen to touch him. A weary, weary smile spread over her lips. "I can see you, Dan."

"Where are you? I'm coming to get you. Just wait. It'll be okay. I promise."

"Dan . . ." Amy shook her head.

"I promise!" Dan yelled.

The image disappeared into a cloud of static and the speakers rose to a deafening, mind-tearing buzz, as if a million hornets had been freed.

"Amy!"

She was shouting; he caught the edges of her words, but she sounded so far away, as if her cries were coming out from some fathomless depth. The screen jolted back into focus.

"Dan? Are you there?"

"I'm here! Right here!"

Amy bit her lip, like he'd seen her do a million times before and hadn't thought anything of it; but it was such an Amy thing that now, at this very moment, he realized he was crying.

Her gaze hardened. "I know why Nathaniel wants the clues. I know what he's planning."

"I don't care about the clues, Amy. Just get somewhere safe!"

"They're all that matter." She smiled. "Only you can stop him. It was always down to you."

"No, that's not true. It's both of us, Amy. I can't do it without you."

The image shook. Amy glanced to the side, off screen, and gasped. "He's coming."

"Run, Amy! Run and hide! I'm coming!"

She stopped, her lips not quite forming her words. Amy's gaze lifted. There was a flicker of fear in the way her eyes widened and the small gasp that caught in her throat. "No . . ."

A crack like a gunshot burst through the speakers.

Dan froze. "Amy?" he whispered.

The cell, fallen from Amy's hands, faced up at a ceiling.

Someone lifted it. As it moved, Dan caught a half-second glimpse of Amy lying on the floor.

Alek Spasky appeared. His eyes narrowed with curiosity as he peered into the phone's camera. "Nathaniel? Are you there?"

"What have you done to my sister?" Dan could barely form the words.

"Nathaniel?"

"What have you done to Amy?" Dan yelled.

It can't be. She can't be . . .

He couldn't finish the thought. He couldn't allow it.

"I'm here, Alek," said Nathaniel, taking the phone from Dan's numb fingers.

"It's done," replied Alek, quite casually. "The Cahill girl is dead."

CHAPTER 1

Ian Kabra's private apartment, London
Three days earlier . . .

Ian closed his eyes and allowed the scent of the tea to rise up gently, temptingly, through his nostrils. He sighed happily.

Now this *is how tea should be brewed.*

Ian leaned back into his chair, enclosing the cup with both hands, letting the tea's aroma envelop him.

The tea tasted so much *better* now. Why?

Because he was no longer leader of the Cahills. He'd unburdened himself of all the dreary responsibilities of the family, and he felt . . . reborn.

He'd been up early, before the others, and strolled, breathing in deep the London air. It was sharp and heavy and delicious. He'd watched the trees in Hyde Park, full of early-summer blooms, and been dazzled by the vast palette of colors.

Now, breakfast. Not the hurried toast snatched and bitter coffee gulped down as mere fuel for the body, but freshly made croissants and this . . . divine cup of tea, all to be savored, enjoyed.

He was glad he'd been leader, despite the disasters. Glad because it made him appreciate all the little things. Appreciate them properly.

He opened his eyes slowly and met Cara's amused gaze.

"Honestly, Kabra, it's just boiled water and some leaves." She poured half a jug of milk into hers and added a heaped spoonful of sugar.

The absolute best thing about surrendering leadership?

That kiss she'd given him right after. He hoped there'd be another soon.

And the worst thing?

Dan and Amy being in charge. Again.

And arguing. Again.

Maybe that was why Nellie and Sammy were taking so long getting the croissants. They'd left ages ago.

Dan was sitting at the kitchen table, fists clenched and glaring at his sister on the opposite side. "We should go after Nathaniel. No more messing around."

Amy groaned. Ian could see her exasperation. He knew that look all too well. He'd seen it in every mirror every day he'd lived at the Cahill mansion. "Let me explain once more for the hard of thinking," started Amy. "We have to assume Nathaniel has found the ingredients for the serum. All he needs is the formula. Which is in that thick head of yours, Dan! So you sit this one out!"

Dan rose from his chair and leaned halfway across the table. "I am a part of this team and I want to help take down the Outcast!"

Amy sprang up. "Over my dead body!"

Ian looked around as the others gathered. They were all together again, at his apartment just off Hatton Garden. All of them safe, for now.

Rain splashed against the window, the drops sparkling on the glass, as if the sky were crying diamonds. Despite the gloomy grayness of the skies, London still looked beautiful. The streets were shiny with puddles, and the leaves on the trees that lined the streets were as glossy as emeralds.

Diamonds and emeralds were what Hatton Garden was famous for. It was a street of jewelers, hidden behind the old lawyer domain of the Temple. He'd passed a couple this morning, huddled under an umbrella, admiring the rings in the window. He saw how they had their arms wrapped around each other under the protection of the umbrella, keeping the outside world at bay with their own closeness. The idea of being that close to someone, trusting them so much, was new to him. New, and a little bit frightening.

He looked over to the opposite sofa.

Cara sat with one leg tucked under the other, chin resting on her knee. She leaned her head slightly, as if she could listen better, see the world better, at an angle.

She looked at him, and there was a clever, maybe too clever, smile on her lips, as if she was on the verge of laughing.

Ian stiffened. *Laughing at me, as usual.*

Was he that comical?

His tie wasn't straight. That would not do.

Ham was on to his third (or was it his fourth?) burger. Jonah's fingers twitched nervously on the remote and his eyes kept switching to the blank screen up on the wall. That was the world he lived in, and he couldn't keep away from it forever. Being out of the media spotlight for a week was like being away from your job for a decade in real years. Ian met Jonah's eyes; Jonah shrugged and put the remote back on the table.

There was a loud, window-shaking burp from the sofa.

Ham blushed, then grinned. "Better out than in, right?"

"Wrong," muttered Ian. He lowered his teacup. The joy had gone. He glanced over at Ham's own breakfast.

Who but Ham would start the day with burgers?

"What I don't get is why he wants the clues at all," said Ham. He rolled up the rest of his burger and pushed it into his ever-so-wide jaw. "Muumph mumm ummph."

Ian watched the bits of bun and diced onions tumble down Ham's T-shirt and onto his

Turkmenian carpet. Early nineteenth century. If he remembered correctly, this one had come out of a little dacha near Kiev, right after the collapse of the Soviet Union. He sighed a little, he died a little. It wasn't just a carpet, it was history. He glared at Ham. "Do you mind?"

Ham pointed at his mouth. "Whhump uhmm?"

"No, I don't want some. You do know that's processed meat? Forty-three percent of it is actually—oh, never mind." Ian whipped out his handkerchief, marched over, and tucked it into Ham's collar, just in time to catch a drip of ketchup.

Ham reached for another burger.

Ian grabbed the tray. "First explain what you meant."

Ham's gaze fell longingly at the pile of juicy food. "Nathaniel's, like, really old. Wrinkly-crinkly old. How long has he got? Five years? Ten with a healthy diet and exercise? The serum makes you crazy-smart and strong but doesn't extend your lifespan."

"No, it doesn't, it actually makes it shorter," said Amy. "Maybe he wants to give it to someone else? Someone younger who'll continue his legacy?"

Dan shook his head. "He doesn't come across as the kind of guy who shares his toys."

"Whatever he wants it for, we know it's not for anything good," said Ian. "Which brings us neatly around to the problem at hand." He looked across at the younger Cahill. "And that is, what to do with you, Dan?"

"Forget it," said Dan, looking over at his sister. "The plan stinks and I'm not going along with it."

"Dan, be reasonable. . . ." said Amy.

"No," snapped Dan.

"If Nathaniel gets his hands on you, Dan, then he has all the clues. He's won," continued Ian. "Have I lost anyone yet, or are we all clear?"

Double thumbs-up from Ham.

"Amy's plan is simple," said Ian. "Keep you safe, and force Nathaniel to waste time and resources looking for you. You're bait, but you're safe. And while he's busy doing that, we can be working to stop him, once and for all."

Cara nodded. "And the system's up and ready. We know Nathaniel's using the Cahill satellite and facial recognition software. What we need to do is have it working for us. A hack would be noticed, so we need to be subtle."

Cara walked up to Dan and put her arms around him. "We need to have Dan's pretty face showing up throughout the world." She ruffled his hair.

Dan frowned but didn't stop her. "How?"

Cara pinched his cheek. "I've downgraded the facial recognition software's accuracy. Not too much because that would be obvious—just to eighty-five percent."

"Huh?" said Ham.

Ian took over. "Face recognition is all about finding unique facial features of the target. Bone structure, eye color, skin pigmentation. The shape of his or her ears. Nathaniel is looking for Dan, but there must be thousands of young men who sort of look like him. Cara's reset the accuracy, so, on a typical day, there'll be a dozen or so triggers. The software will fit young men in Paris. In Moscow. In Nicaragua and Ulan Bator. Nathaniel will have to spread his forces out to try to verify which, if any, is the real Dan."

Dan scowled at his sister. "So that's what you meant about using me as bait?"

Amy drew out a folder and put it gently on the dining room table. "We can't let Nathaniel get his hands on you, Dan. You have no idea what he's capable of."

Ian looked at the folder, its cover wrinkled with age.

They'd found Grace's secret blackmail files. The dirt she'd collected on her own family, all so she could maintain control of the Cahill organization. What was worse was that if she couldn't find any dirt, she'd invent it. But some of it was all too true.

"I think it's about time we realized what sort of monster our grandfather is," said Amy, pushing the file toward Dan. "And why Grace ordered his death."

CHAPTER 2

Amy saw the blood drain from Dan's face as he looked through the folder.

It was time he knew.

That they all knew.

An awful silence dominated the room. Eventually, Dan looked up. "Tell them, Amy."

Amy nodded. "Nathaniel worked for US military research, not surprising for an Ekat. He helped on the Manhattan Project, then became head of research in West Germany. Mom would spend a few weeks a year in West Berlin, visiting him. Grace was too busy to accompany her, of course."

Ian gazed warily at the folder, as if what was in there might poison him. In a way, he was right. "And?"

"Mom would be sent off with her nanny to go see the sights. Have ice cream. Visit the zoo. She was little, only six. But this diary in here . . ." Amy drew out a sheet of paper.

"Your mom's?" asked Ian.

"Yes. It's dated February 12, 1967." The handwriting was neat, and heavy. There were cross-outs, and the stiff letters appeared as separate little soldiers on the page.

"What's it say?" asked Ham. "Read it out loud, Amy."

Amy took a deep breath and started.

"'I am so bored! Daddy never takes me anywhere! He goes off in a big black car, and the driver is a soldier. He does lots of salutes and stuff to Daddy. Daddy is very, very important. I think Mom runs America and Daddy is in charge of Europe. Which is nice, I suppose. If I had to be in charge I think I would want to run Disneyland.'"

Jonah laughed. "Me too. I wanted to run Disneyland when I was six."

Amy continued. "'I am going to go to work with Daddy. I want to see how he runs the country. I've asked before and he got angry and said it wasn't a place for little children, but I will sneak in the trunk when no one is looking. I must make sandwiches.'"

Ian scowled. "That's it?"

Amy pointed to a typed page. "There's a psychiatrist's report, dated a month after, when Mom was back in Attleboro. Weight loss. Bad dreams. Anxiety attacks. Periods of mutism. The conclusion is she'd suffered some deep psychological trauma."

Dan joined her and looked through the next collection. "This is all in Grace's handwriting."

"Read on, Dan," said Amy.

Dan did. "'Hope's turned from a happy-go-lucky

child who wants for nothing into a little mouse who screams at night and is terrified that someone might hurt her pets! I've spoken to Nathaniel again about it, and he says he doesn't know what the problem is. I've decided to take Hope away for a few days. A change of scene may make her open up.' "

Dan looked through the next few pages. "This next entry is some weeks later." He cleared his throat. Amy spotted it, even if the others hadn't—the slight tremble of Dan's hand as he held up this last, fateful sheet.

The words on the paper were few but explained Nathaniel's hatred toward them, and his deadly plan for revenge.

If only Grace had found another way . . .

She saw Dan and the others watching her, waiting for her. Amy smiled. "Go on, Dan."

Dan cleared his throat. " 'I thought I knew Nathaniel. My God, the things he's done. The driver explained it all, once I'd threatened him. Hope smuggled herself into the car. They went off to Nathaniel's laboratory in the Black Forest. I'd known about it, of course, but thought it was low-grade research and development. Building a better bullet, as it were.

" 'I had no idea how far he'd take things in his attempt to re-create his own version of the serum. The methods he'd use. They are monstrous.' "

"That's it?" said Jonah. "All he's been after is the serum? He couldn't get it off Grace so he decided to try to make his own version. We should have known."

Dan waved his sheet. "Can I continue?"

"Stage is all yours, bro."

"Thanks," said Dan. " 'I cannot bear to imagine what she saw in Nathaniel's laboratories. Nathaniel threatened her, telling her awful things would happen if she told anyone about his work. That I would not understand.

" 'How wrong he is. I understand perfectly. No wonder Nathaniel was so desperate. The truth of what he's doing in that research facility will destroy him.

" 'And no one hurts my child.' "

Amy opened up the folder and spread out the other documents. "It's not just letters and reports in there. There's an old military map, with an area circled in red. It's all in German, but it looks like it's in the Black Forest. There was a report, too." Amy picked that up.

" 'The facility has been destroyed, but Nathaniel has fled. The secrets will now lie buried in that awful place forever. Secrets that could destroy us all and terrorize the world if anyone attempted to replicate them.' "

Ham grunted. "Now, that doesn't sound good."

Amy read on. " 'I cannot let my personal feelings get in the way of what must be done to protect my family. Nathaniel must have known it would come to this. He must be removed, permanently, lest he rebuild his research facility again, and farther away from innocent eyes.

"'I shall find a way to explain it to Hope. That her father is gone.'"

Amy held up a short telegram, dated November 5, 1967. "This is from Vladimir Spasky to Grace."

"What's it say?" asked Jonah.

"'Nathaniel Hartford is dead.'"

CHAPTER 3

Argument over.

But they still didn't have a plan, exactly.

Ian needed some fresh air and time alone to think. But three steps out of the apartment and he walked into a puddle. It was deeper than he'd expected.

Drat. Those were cashmere socks.

"Ian! Wait!" Cara flipped up the collar of her rain-coat and cast a wary eye at the clouds overhead.

Ian glanced at his soaked-through shoes. *Why is it, when I do something stupid, Cara is always around?*

"Yes?" he replied, more testily than he wanted to.

"What's wrong?"

"Never mind."

Cara scowled. "Fine. If you want to go rushing off by yourself, then go right ahead. What is it? Tea with the Queen?"

"Don't be ridiculous—it's only ten." Ian tapped his watch. "Tea's at four."

"Was that . . . a joke?" She shook her head. "Ian Kabra made a joke."

"I think that's classed as a witticism. A joke has

more the traditional 'a horse walks into a bar' type of structure," Ian replied.

Cara laughed. She threw her head back and her hair shook. It was good watching her. Ian smiled as she covered her mouth, embarrassed at how loud she was being.

Ian didn't care.

Life couldn't be so bad if he could make Cara laugh like that.

"This is Lunt's," said Ian, opening the narrow black door. "They've been serving coffee here since the seventeenth century, and it's the only place in London you can get a decent cappuccino." He nodded to the waitress and led Cara to a table.

"How did you find this place?" Cara asked.

"Father used to bring me here, back in . . . better days." Ian inspected the furnishings. Patchy armchairs, plain wooden stools, bare floorboards. Yet it was warm, and the smell of the different beans took him back to a happy memory. "He brought me here for my birthday once. Said he'd got something special for me. I was so excited. I'd been on and on at him for a first-edition copy of *The Hobbit*."

Cara's eyebrow arched. "And?"

"It was a book, at least it was that." Ian could still remember the feel of the wrapping paper, the way his heart raced as he tore it. Then the dismal plummeting as he saw the cover. "It was Sun Tzu's *The Art of War*. In the original Chinese."

"Poor, poor Ian."

Cara then sat by the café window, resting her chin on her fist, watching the world hurry by in the rain.

Ian put himself down opposite and followed her gaze.

Typical London. People hidden under their umbrellas, plenty scurrying with newspapers over their heads to protect them from the heavy rain-drops. It amazed Ian that still happened. This was England. How could you step out the door without an umbrella?

Across the road was a covered bus stop. A lone middle-aged businessman waited, chin sunk deep into his raised collar, hands stuffed into his pockets. He looked over at the café.

Warm and dry in here, chum.

Ian sipped his cappuccino. Everything about the café invited them to linger. But they weren't in London for the diamonds of Hatton Garden.

"Well, Ian?"

"Well what?"

"I can see you thinking. What's your plan?"

Ian straightened his cuffs. Was that chocolate on the edge? He'd told the waitress to be careful. "Ah, yes. The plan. Nathaniel's given us very few options, and that's good. This time."

"How is having fewer options good?"

"He's attacked the Janus branch. He's all but wiped out mine, the Lucians. And from Nellie and

Sammy's visit to Mount Fuji we know the Tomas have been . . . neutralized. That leaves . . . ?"

"The Ekat branch." Cara nodded.

"Exactly. The Ekats. Our very own band of boffins." Ian had spent the whole trip from Rotterdam looking at the angles. The more he thought about it, the more a pattern emerged. "His next disaster will be to eliminate that branch."

Cara frowned. "But Nathaniel's an Ekat. Why would he wipe out his own branch?"

"He is the Outcast, Cara. Think what that means. He has no loyalty to any part of the Cahill organization and, as Dan put it, he's not the sort of fellow who shares his toys. No, this next disaster will be the biggest, and it will be aimed at the Ekats, I'm certain."

"What's his strategy, then?"

"To get the Ekats together. With all that's been happening they'll be wary, so it'll be something they can't resist, and given how long Nathaniel's been planning this, I'll bet it's been on the calendar for quite a while."

"Do you know what it is?"

"No, but I know a man who might. Professor Peerless, a lecturer at Imperial College London."

Cara smiled. "I get it. There, or MIT, right?"

"Right. Imperial is one of the most prestigious science colleges in the world and has an above-average presence of Ekats on its faculty, the professor being one of them." Ian glanced at his watch. "And he's expecting us for brunch."

Cara's smile widened. There were creases at the edge of her eyes.

Ian blushed. "What are you staring at?" He put his hand to his mouth. "I've froth on my lip, haven't I? All this time we've been talking and I've been wearing a foam mustache."

Cara took his hand and lowered it. She put it down on the table and tucked her fingers around his.

Why *was* she looking at him like that?

That laugh of hers tinkled in the back of her throat. "Ian Kabra, what am I going to do with you?"

"Ian Kabra, what am I going to do with you?"

Alek Spasky switched off the sound recorder. He had all he needed.

Love makes you blind.

Ian had looked right at him. If the boy hadn't been so distracted by the young woman opposite, he would have realized something was off.

Perhaps Vikram Kabra was right, the boy was too soft to be a true Lucian. He'd also been right about the coffeehouse—sooner or later Ian would go there. Alek found it interesting how willing Vikram was to betray his own son. To Alek, family was all.

The Cahills were responsible for his sister's death, so they, too, must die. It was simple family loyalty.

Alek gripped the Makarov semiautomatic pistol in his pocket, his thumb idly resting on the safety.

He could cross the road and finish them both now. They were so deep in each other's eyes they hadn't seen him at all. Perhaps that would be a kindness. Their last moments of life would be happy ones.

No, that would put the rest of them on alert and he'd lose the other boy, Dan Cahill.

The bus slowed down and Alek reluctantly released his hold on his weapon. He missed his ring darts but, as his old KGB instructor once warned him, over-reliance on a single weapon was a sign of weakness, and vanity.

He drew out his wallet and smiled at the bus driver. "Excuse me, but does this go to Imperial College?"

CHAPTER 4

Imperial College London

Dr. Peerless looked disappointedly at his doughnut.

They're definitely getting smaller every year.

He sighed, took a bite, and admired the view from the top of Queen's Tower.

This was all that remained of the original college. A neat, brick tower on a lawn surrounded by cutting-edge laboratories, massive lecture theaters, and modern dormitories.

He'd been coming here since his first days as an undergraduate, oh, a long time ago now. He and his mates would sneak to the top of the tower for a break, looking out over the college and South Kensington itself, boasting of the things they'd accomplish.

Dr. Peerless looked at his wrinkled hands. How could that bright, hopeful boy have turned into this decrepit old man?

Still, from those days on, every day up he'd marched, taking all the steps even when they'd installed the elevator, to look over his kingdom. And have a doughnut.

True, the steps wearied him more than ever and he now had to stop three times before he reached the top, but the view was always worth it.

It made him young again, just for a while.

He took a second bite, savoring the strawberry jam that seeped out of the heart of the doughnut. He tried to lick it off before it dripped, but was too late. A splotch fell onto his white shirt.

"Blast." He searched his pocket for a napkin.

"Use this."

The voice emerged out of the shadowy doorway. Peerless turned to see a man, his raincoat shiny with raindrops. He held out a handkerchief.

Dr. Peerless squinted. He'd left his glasses in the laboratory, too. Getting old and forgetful. "The tower is closed to students."

"I'm not a student."

Dr. Peerless took the handkerchief. "It's not open to the public, either."

The man leaned his elbows on the edge of the arched opening. "That's a shame. The view is splendid."

Dr. Peerless nodded as he joined him. The first rush of sugar had put him in a good mood. Let his handkerchief-carrying savior stay. "That it is." He glanced over. "Russian?"

The man smiled. "I thought I'd lost my accent a long time ago."

"I spent quite a while in Russia and Ukraine, or

the Soviet Union as it was then, after the Chernobyl disaster."

"A bad time," the man said.

Peerless nodded. "The worst. Terrifying."

He still dreamed about it, even after all these years. Back in 1986 he'd just been promoted to head of nuclear technology and his first job was to help at what was the world's worst nuclear disaster. The reactor at Chernobyl had overheated and exploded, hurling a radioactive cloud over much of Europe.

"Nuclear meltdowns are your field of work?"

Dr. Peerless shook his head. "Contamination. It was my job to map out dispersion patterns, radiation levels in the soil. Track levels of radiation poisoning and mutation." He shook his head, remembering some of the awful things he'd seen. "That was then. Now I specialize in green technology. To try to free us from our"—he glanced at his doughnut—"bad habits."

The man laughed. "You seek to save the world?"

Dr. Peerless grinned. The young man he'd once been had promised himself he'd do exactly that. "That's one way of looking at it. Why else become a scientist if not to make the world a better place?"

"A sentiment worthy of an Ekat."

Dr. Peerless tensed. "A what?"

The man shook his head. "You are not a fool, Dr. Peerless, please do not assume I am one."

Dr. Peerless only now noticed the man was wearing tight black gloves. It made him afraid in a way he hadn't been in years. When he'd first arrived at Chernobyl, they'd often been "chaperoned" by men in raincoats with tight black gloves. The power station had been built in Ukraine, one of the republics that made up the old Soviet Union. Then, one night at the end, over a bottle of vodka, he'd been told who they were. . . .

"KGB," whispered Dr. Peerless. The doughnut fell from his hands.

"It was a tradition to give the condemned man one last meal," said the man as he approached Peerless.

CHAPTER 5

"The traffic's a nightmare, mate," said the taxi driver. "You're better off walking. Imperial's just five minutes up the road."

"What's holding us up? Can you tell?" asked Ian, irritated. They'd been stuck at the traffic light for five minutes now, unable to move because of the gridlock.

The taxi driver shrugged.

Ian flicked out a twenty-pound note. "Keep the change."

He and Cara hit Exhibition Road. Monolithic marble-clad buildings lined either side and were guarded by statues of mythic heroes and preeminent Britons.

Cara gazed around. "Wow. I feel like I'm in a Sherlock Holmes movie."

Ian didn't understand. "It's just Exhibition Road." He must have walked it a thousand times when going from the shops on Kensington High Street down to Harrods for more shopping. Really, it was the only place worth shopping. Its food hall was world famous and the only place west of St. Petersburg that sold decent caviar.

"What's that?" asked Cara.

"The Natural History Museum."

"That?"

"The Science Museum."

"And that?"

"The Victoria and Albert Museum."

"And that?"

"Kensington Gardens and yes, that's Kensington Palace and the big dome is the Albert Hall." He started off. "But we're in a hurry."

They passed the Royal Geographical Society and the solemn statues of great explorers. As they turned the corner into Imperial, Ian saw the ambulances.

And the police cars.

"Quickly," he ordered.

Cara nodded and they both ran toward the flashing lights and the gathering crowd.

"What's going on?" Cara asked.

A student turned around. "There's been an accident. They say someone's fallen from Queen's Tower."

"Do you know who?" asked Ian, though his sinking gut warned him he already knew.

Another student piped up. "One of the professors. The tower's been shut for ages, loose masonry. Old fool must have lost his footing."

Ian gazed up at the tower. "You don't think . . . ?"

"Yes, I do. Dr. Peerless isn't going to make his appointment."

"Oh. Now what? He was my only lead."

Cara grabbed Ian's arm. "Come on."

"Where?"

"Dr. Peerless's office." Cara dragged him through the crowd toward the department building. "And we need to be quick."

They entered the Mechanical Engineering building, straight past security guards who were too busy peering out the windows at the scene on the lawn. The police had moved the crowd back and there were medics at the base of the tower. People pointed at the viewing platform of the tower. It had been a long way down.

They got in the elevator and Cara jammed a button. "We need his appointment schedule."

"A man like Peerless will have hundreds of appointments. What are we looking for?" asked Ian. Things were going too quickly and he needed a moment to plan, think things through.

But Cara was in a hurry. She tapped her foot impatiently as she watched the floor indicator lights slowly ascend. "It'll be an invitation that seems too good to be true. And it may have been cc'd to a lot of other people, the majority being Ekats."

Ian frowned. "The police will be up here in minutes. We can't be caught hacking a murdered man's e-mails."

Cara smiled as the doors opened. "Leave that to me."

The corridor was lined with anonymous office doors. There was no natural lighting and the walls were mere plasterboard, but someone had put in the effort to add a few potted plants and colorful landscape photographs. Cara could hear . . . sobbing?

"Someone's inside," she said.

"Let me deal with this." Ian knocked on the door marked DR. PEERLESS.

A secretary sat, sniffing into a tissue, phone cradled on her shoulder. She blinked through tear-smeared glasses. "I'm—I'm sorry, but the office is closed today. There's been an accident."

"Not an accident," said Ian, "but a tragedy." He handed over his silk handkerchief. The secretary took it and blew long and hard into it. Ian stared at the soaking cloth, his face wrinkled in disgust. "A terrible tragedy." He took her hand and looked softly into the secretary's eyes. "I've been sent by the dean. It's unfair for you to stay here, given what's happened. Take the rest of the day off."

"What?" asked the secretary.

"If it helps, Harrods is having a sale. End of season on"—he glanced at her—"Dior and Hermès." Ian helped her smoothly from her chair and handed the secretary her handbag. "I wouldn't rush in tomorrow, either."

"Are you sure the dean—"

"It's at least fifty percent off on scarves. But I'd hurry." Ian helped her put on her coat. "Don't worry, I'll lock up."

He led her out the door and waved her off until she was in the elevator. Then Ian closed the door and locked it.

"What. Was. That?" said Cara.

"That was pure charm," said Ian. "Do you have a data stick?"

"I always have a data stick. And I don't believe it," said Cara, inserting the data stick. "The woman's boss has just died and you send her shopping?"

"I sent her to Harrods, there's a difference," Ian replied.

"All done." The data stick went into Cara's pocket. "Let's go."

Heels clacked on the corridor floor.

Ian jolted to a stop by the door. "Hold on. Someone's coming."

They didn't have the almost telepathic empathy of Dan and Amy, but they knew danger when it was about to knock on the door.

Cara pointed to the window. It was half open.

Ian shook his head and mouthed, *Are you insane? We're five stories up.*

Cara stabbed her finger at the window again.

Then they heard a slow slide and click.

Ian paled.

He didn't have a huge amount of experience with firearms, but it sounded a lot like a bullet being chambered.

Cara slid out and grabbed the upper ledge. Chest

against the wall, she shuffled along to make way for him. "Come on!"

The good thing about these grand Victorian buildings were the window ledges. The wide window ledges. And the buttresses. And the statues. So many handholds and places to hide. It was almost impossible to fall off. Except when it had been raining. The marble was as slippery as oil on ice.

Ian stared down and went a mix of pale and sickly. Each floor was about fifteen feet high and there were five of them between him and some very hard-looking paving slabs. He did a quick calculation. Seventy-five feet.

He stepped out with one trembling leg.

The doorknob turned.

Ian thrust his other leg onto the ledge. He closed his eyes and whispered a little prayer. Ian's shoes were Church's, with handmade leather soles designed so they wouldn't leave prints on expensive carpets. They were not designed for scrambling around on ledges. He swallowed and shuffled out very carefully.

The office door opened.

Papers rustled, and they could both hear drawers being opened and closed. The searcher was taking his, or her, time.

Ian heard the clicking of keys and the soft hum of a hard drive.

A cell phone rang, and for an awful moment Ian

thought it was his. Then, with great relief, he realized it was coming from within the office.

"Da?"

Cara flashed Ian a panicked look. It was Alek Spasky. He was the man in the office.

Ian leaned in to hear more and his foot slipped away. He scrabbled with his right hand and caught nothing but air.

But Cara grabbed him.

Ian swung off the ledge, clasping her fingers. He dangled there, seventy-five feet up with only Cara's slim fingers between him and a splattery death. His heart thumped high in his throat while his stomach dropped down to his toes.

Cara had managed to hook her other arm around the neck of a statue. But Ian could see her grip failing.

What would give first? His hold on Cara, or her hold on the statue?

She needs to let me go, thought Ian. *But she won't.*

Ian met her gaze and opened his hand.

"Don't. You. Dare," Cara hissed, locking her grip even tighter.

"Of course the bomb is in place, Nathaniel," continued Alek. "Now I must go to Kiev. To Natalia."

Kiev? What business did Alek have in Kiev?

"Do not presume to order me, Nathaniel. I assist you, but I do not *serve* you." There was no mistaking the anger in Alek's voice. The phone clicked off.

Ian gritted his teeth. The ground loomed beneath him.

One look at Cara warned Ian she was hurting badly. Her face was sweaty and red with effort, and her arms were shaking.

Hinges. A lock clicking. "He's gone," Cara hissed. "Climb up."

With a pained gasp, Cara swung him to the ledge, and Ian clambered onto her legs, then her waist, and up around her chest.

"Watch it!" Cara yelped.

"What?" Ian blushed as he realized. "Oh, I'm—"

"The window, Ian. Just get in through the window."

Finally, the two of them reentered the office. The computer screen had been swept off the desk and lay cracked on the floor. Cara picked it up and plugged it back in.

"I don't admit to knowing Alek Spasky well," she said as she rebooted. "But he seemed very angry with Nathaniel, don't you think?"

"*Very.*" Now, that was something. "Any discord between allies has to be exploited. I read that in Sun Tzu."

The screen, cracked as it was, flickered to life.

"What was he looking for?" asked Ian.

Cara inspected the computer. A few quick taps on the keyboard and her suspicions were confirmed. "He deleted some e-mails. Neat. If he'd wiped the whole disk it would have been suspicious. So he just picked the ones he needed and got rid of them."

"But you've got them, right?"

She tapped her hip pocket. "Oh, yes. I've got them."

CHAPTER 6

Dan shoved his jeans into his backpack, punching them down to the very bottom.

Jonah raised an eyebrow. "What's that pair of Levi's ever done to you?"

Dan glowered at him. He was too angry to speak so he grabbed his hoodie, rolled it up, and rammed that in, too.

Jonah returned to scanning his tablet.

"This sucks," Dan declared.

"Yup," said Jonah, his gaze still locked on the screen.

"You're not helping." Dan threw a shoe at Jonah. Anything to stop him from looking at the tablet.

Ham snatched it out of the air inches from Jonah's head.

Jonah fist-bumped Ham. "You're the man."

Ham tossed the shoe seamlessly into Dan's open backpack. "You know it."

Dan scowled. "How would you two like it? Being pushed off the team?"

Jonah put the tablet down and swung his feet off the chair. He leaned forward, elbows on his knees, to get a good, hard look at Dan. "Amy and our boy in pink cashmere are right. Nathaniel wants you, Dan. Or at least what's locked in your head."

The formula for the serum.

Dan's photographic memory trapped in his brain the process of combining the thirty-nine ingredients to create the serum. He couldn't get rid of it if he tried. And he had.

Amy stood at the door with her arms crossed in her "big sister" mode. "Hey, Dan." She'd probably send him to live in a monastery in Tibet if it kept him safe.

Jonah nudged Ham. "Oh, yeah, I suddenly remembered. We've got to do that . . . thing."

Ham blinked. "What thing?"

Jonah grabbed Ham's arm "That *thing*, Ham."

Amy closed the door behind them. "Could they be any more obvious?" She looked around at the scattered clothes. "You okay?"

"I'm about a million miles from okay."

"Nellie and Sammy are back. They've agreed to the plan. The three of you are going to Madrid. Nellie has family there; it'll be safe."

"What about you? And the rest of the guys?" Deep down, he knew his sister was right. He was a liability to the entire team. They couldn't work if they were constantly looking over their shoulders, worrying about him. But all he'd do is spend his days worrying about *them*.

"One team will deal with the threat to the Ekats, once we figure out what it is. The other will head off to the Black Forest. Grace was terrified about what had happened there. We have to find out if Nathaniel's picked up from where he left off."

"You think he'd still be using this research facility?"

Amy shook her head. "No, not after all this time. But whatever his plan is, it's connected with what he was doing there back in the nineteen sixties. There's a big piece of the puzzle missing, Dan. A secret Grace herself said would *destroy* Nathaniel. And we'll find it in the Black Forest."

CHAPTER 7

Ian stopped at the door to Cara's room. "This is the door to your room."

Cara replied, "Yes . . . ?"

"Why don't we work downstairs? The dining table's large enough for your laptop."

Cara frowned. She did that a lot with him. "But my laptop's in here and it's plugged in and has a hard drive and booster and it's next to the cookie jar? The one with the lilies painted on it?"

"That's not a cookie jar. That's a seventeenth-century Ming dynasty—"

"*Whatever*, Kabra. Just get in here." Cara huffed and pushed him in. "Find yourself a chair. And grab yourself a cookie."

Cara had settled in, that was for sure. Clothes lay in messy piles on the carpet and various backs of chairs. Laundry hung off clothes hangers from doorways, and there, screen glowing and right next to the antique porcelain Ming dynasty *cookie jar*, was her laptop.

Ian stopped as he saw the bed. "And what are those?"

"My . . . er, trolls."

He stared at the neon-haired plastic monstrosities. "What are these abominations doing in my apartment?"

"I like them. I take them everywhere. It makes anyplace a home. Even a place like this."

Ian almost choked until he saw her smirk. She tossed the data stick from one hand to another. "Enough about decorating, Ian. Let's get to work."

The data stick went in, and a few seconds later the e-mail box was up and open. "Tsk. Hardly any security at all. What's the fun in that?" Cara clicked, clicked, and clicked away. "Nope. Nope. Nope. Definitely not." The screen cast its glow over her sculpted features, added deeper shadows under her cheeks and an electric shine to her eyes. "It's mostly just assignments from students. Schedules. Lab results. Oh, and an invitation to the dean's summer party."

"Maybe that's it! Alek mentioned a bomb. Perhaps he's planning to do it then? Kill the faculty staff?"

"Hardly the Outcast's style. He'd want something bigger, don't you think?"

"Yes. Nathaniel does seem to have a taste for the dramatic."

Cara froze. "How about a trip to China?"

"Well, perhaps when this is all over a week or two—"

"No! Peerless was invited to China. Shanghai, to be specific. A symposium on future technology. It's called Saving the World through Science." Cara clicked open the attachment. "Whoa. First-class flight. Five-star hotel. Talks on . . . pretty much everything. It's Ekat bait. Solar power. Biofuels. Wind technology and . . . animal conservation. Monitoring the tiger population in Siberia. Dolphin communication and . . . ha! Saving the bee! Bet someone thought long and hard about that one!"

"Which hotel?" asked Ian.

"The Hilton Shanghai."

Ian checked his cell phone. "Shanghai it is. When does the symposium start?"

"Three days' time."

"I'll go tell the others. You start packing your bags. And trolls." Ian faltered. "Though . . . only if you want to come. I'm not saying you have to."

Cara looked at him as if trying to read his mind. "Only if *you* want me to come. You could take . . . you know, one of the others. . . ."

"You want me to go with someone else?" Ian asked, frowning. "I suppose Amy would be interested. Keep her distracted from missing Dan."

Cara set her lips in a thin line. "Yes. That's a great idea. Take Amy."

Somehow the conversation had taken an unexpected detour and Ian couldn't quite figure out where. "You don't want to go?"

"You're taking Amy. You just said so." Cara hit the mouse hard to close the screen. "I don't care."

"Fine," said Ian. "I will."

"Fine," replied Cara, slamming the laptop shut. "Go ahead."

Ian stood up. "And by the way, that's a chamber pot, not a cookie jar."

CHAPTER 8

"You think Nathaniel is planning to bomb the symposium?" asked Amy. "Something that simple?"

They were all back in the living room. Nellie and Sammy on the sofa together; Ham by the fridge, hoovering up whatever was left of breakfast, Dan helping him; and Jonah glued to the television. Cara and Ian were at totally opposite sides of the room. Ian shifted uncomfortably, and Cara was staring daggers at him.

Whatever it is, Amy thought, *I don't want to know.*

"I doubt it will be simple," said Ian. "But Alek went to an extraordinary amount of trouble to hide all the Shanghai details from us, and that included tossing a Nobel Prize–winning scientist off a tall tower, so I'm certain Shanghai is the target."

"I've looked through the list of invitees," Cara added. "Three-quarters of them are Ekats."

Amy agreed. "Shanghai it is. But a bomb? It doesn't match Nathaniel's theme. If he plans to take out the Ekats he'd want to re-create some historical disaster, like he did with the three others."

Ham held up three fingers. *"Titanic. Hindenburg.* Katrina. Check."

"So what'll be the fourth?" asked Dan.

Jonah raised the remote. "Maybe he'll tell us. Alek Spasky is on the news."

"What?" exclaimed Amy.

Jonah raised the volume on the news report on Dr. Peerless's death.

The TV crew was interviewing some students while an ambulance and police worked in the background. A picture of the Queen's Tower was inserted in the top left of the screen with the banner TRAGIC ACCIDENT ROBS BRITAIN OF NOBEL PRIZE–WINNING SCIENTIST. There was a crowd watching the action on the lawn at the foot of the tower.

Jonah leaned forward. "Don't you see him? At the back?" He paused the clip. "Look."

Everyone was looking toward the lawn, except one man. He was looking at the screen, at the viewer.

At us.

Alek Spasky.

"For a spy he's not trying very hard to stay hidden," suggested Ham. "Don't they teach that at spy school?"

Amy shook her head. "No, he wanted us to see him. But why?"

Jonah furrowed his brow. "Behind him . . ."

"A wall?" said Ham.

"What's on the wall?"

Amy stared at Ham, who looked back equally confused.

Jonah walked up to the screen. "See that poster? What's it say?"

Amy leaned forward. Alek was leaning up against the wall, right next to the poster, smiling.

"It's a concert. Scheduled for three days from now. The Cities in Dust tour." She looked at Jonah. "So?"

Jonah sighed. " 'Cities in Dust' is a song by Siouxsie and the Banshees." Jonah drew a circle around the image of a dark-haired woman. "The poster is a fake. Siouxsie retired years ago."

Cara peered at the glowing picture. "It's another challenge from the Outcast."

Amy bit her lip. Of course it was. Alek was standing there for a reason. He'd *wanted* the camera to catch him. " 'Cities in Dust' doesn't sound very good," she said.

Jonah spoke. "It's about Pompeii, the Roman city destroyed by a volcanic eruption two thousand years ago."

Cara nodded. "Mount Vesuvius. Still active, in case you were wondering."

Amy was afraid. "You think the Outcast is planning a volcanic eruption? How?"

Cara shrugged. "Maybe you could throw a nuke down the crater?"

"The chap's from the Cold War era," suggested Ian. "That sort of thing is his MO."

Amy wasn't convinced. "Jonah, when did the song get released?"

"April 1986. It was from their *Tinderbox* album. I have a first pressing back home."

"Jonah, dig up events during April 1986."

Jonah's thumb danced over his cell. "What am I looking for?"

"'Cities in Dust.' The Outcast had picked that song for a very good reason. . . ."

Jonah stopped. "Uh-oh."

"What?"

He looked up at them, pale. "If this is what he's planning . . ."

"Tell us, Jonah."

"I'm sending it to the TV." Jonah pointed at the big flat-screen. "You'd better see for yourselves."

The image was of a blown-up building. Flames and smoke consumed the sky and the fire trucks and ambulances surrounding it looked small and pathetic compared to the explosion.

"'April 26, 1986,'" said Jonah, reading off the screen. "'Chernobyl, Ukraine. The world's biggest nuclear disaster.'"

They sat silently, staring at the wreckage.

The Outcast had saved the worst for last.

CHAPTER 9

Amy couldn't take her eyes off the screen. The implications of Nathaniel's plan were horrifying.

How could Nathaniel be so consumed with revenge? She saw the looks of horror frozen on the others, all hypnotized by the scale of the disaster.

"He's going to re-create a nuclear meltdown?" asked Ham, eyes huge and fixed on the TV screen. "Can he do that?"

Amy sank back into the sofa. "Of course he can."

Jan looked at Cara. "Find us the nuclear power station nearest to Shanghai."

"On it." Cara flipped open her laptop.

Amy scanned through the report on the screen. She knew about Chernobyl, but it felt like ancient history to her. "One of the reactors overheated and exploded. Covered much of Europe with radioactive dust. Not a major death toll to begin with—staff from the initial explosion and the engineers who sacrificed themselves to shut it down—but the repercussions are with us today. High cancer rates among locals. Mutations in the wildlife. A whole city abandoned."

"What are the chances that Nathaniel will be aiming at something bigger?" Jonah shook his head.

Ian sat down on the coffee table, elbows resting on his knees. "We've got one advantage. Nathaniel expected us to pick up on the Chernobyl hint. He wants us to panic, and nothing generates bigger panic than a nuclear meltdown. He expected us to waste days running around wildly, looking for his target. He doesn't know we know it's Shanghai."

Amy agreed. "So what do we do? Tell everyone? Get the symposium canceled?"

"It would stop Nathaniel's plans for now, but he'd only set it up again and next time we may not be warned."

"We're risking millions of lives," said Amy. "Letting the whole city of Shanghai sit on a nuclear time bomb."

Ian's brown eyes hardened. "Your call, Amy."

She wanted to take out a full-page ad in every newspaper, warning the world of Nathaniel's plan. She wanted to have it on every news channel in every language. She looked over at her superstar cousin. All it would take was a single press announcement from Jonah and the world would know of the Outcast.

But they'd tried that in the Netherlands, and no one had believed them.

"I'm going to Shanghai," said Amy.

Ian nodded. "I'll start packing."

"No," said Amy. "I can't risk you guys. If it goes wrong, I'll need you to be around to stop Nathaniel without me."

Ian frowned. "You know what you're asking?"

Ham stood up. "Seems to me we should decide for ourselves if we're going or not."

Jonah slung his arm over the big guy's shoulder. "Seems to me Ham's right." He looked around the room. "Who's for Shanghai?" He and Ham put their hands up.

So did Ian.

But not Cara. She was frowning at her screen. "A small glitch, guys."

"What is it?" asked Ian, looking over her shoulder.

"There are no nuclear power stations near Shanghai. Certainly not near enough to do the sort of damage we're expecting."

Amy joined Ian. "Are you sure?"

"Yup. Look for yourselves." Cara magnified the map of Shanghai and the area around it. "I've highlighted the stations in red."

The nearest nuclear power station, Qinshan, was hundreds of miles away.

Cara clicked her mouse and a circle grew up around the stations. "Even with a total meltdown, the range of the explosion would be a dozen miles at best. There could be plenty of radioactive material ejected into the atmosphere, but there's no guarantee it would blow in the direction of Shanghai."

Amy looked at Ian. "Is this some sort of double-bluff? Have us looking one way and the danger's somewhere else?"

Cara scowled. "One man knows for certain," she said. "That's Alek Spasky. And he's headed to Ukraine, where Chernobyl is."

Amy rubbed her forehead. "That cannot be a coincidence. But what does it matter? He won't tell us anything."

Ian shook his head. "I'm not so sure. He was going to see someone in Kiev, and it sounded like she means a lot to him. If there's a chance to get him to tell us what the plan is, even a small chance—"

"Small?" interrupted Dan. "You mean microscopic. The guy wants us *dead*, Ian."

Ian met his gaze. "If Nathaniel is planning a nuclear disaster, we've got to follow every lead we've got. And our best lead is Alek and this mystery woman he's going to see."

"Seems to me," said Ham, "we have three missions. The Black Forest, Shanghai, and now Chernobyl."

Amy agreed. "What do you think we should do, Ham?"

Ham started. "You're asking me?" He looked to her, then Dan, then Ian. "Don't we have enough bosses?"

She nodded. "Tell us."

Ham looked around for help. Amy could see the pleading in his eyes as they fell on Jonah, but the superstar just kicked back on the sofa, leaving the stage for the big Tomas.

Ham held up three fingers. "So we need this many teams. One to find out whatever dark secret lies in the Black Forest, the second to go to Chernobyl and question Alek Spasky, and the third to go to Shanghai and try and save the Ekats. Okay?"

Amy smiled. Why had a Tomas never been head of the Cahills? Ham was doing a great job.

Jonah chimed in. "I already volunteered for Shanghai."

Ham grinned as if he'd just won Olympic gold. "Me too."

Sammy sat up. "Nellie and I will head off to Germany and look into this research facility of Nathaniel's."

Amy frowned. "What about Dan? You're supposed to take him to Madrid."

Dan looked at her. She could see the pleading in his eyes. He shrugged, trying to act supercasual. "Sure, Madrid would be great, I'd love to spend the day eating Nellie's paella, but you need three teams. . . ."

Amy didn't like it, but he was right. "Dan goes with Nellie and Sammy," she said.

"YES!" yelled Dan, punching the air. He stopped, embarrassed. "I mean, only if you say so."

Amy grinned. How did she ever think she'd be able to stop him? "I'll go with Jonah and Ham to Shanghai." She looked over at Ian and Cara. "You two are heading for Chernobyl."

Ian looked at Cara. Cara looked at Ian. Then both, with perfect synchronicity, answered.

"Fine."

Dan zipped up his backpack and looked around his bedroom one last time.

Did he have everything?

He couldn't believe it, he was on a mission! All that time they'd argued about him going into hiding didn't matter now. He checked his watch. The taxi would be on its way to take him, Nellie, and Sammy to the airport.

He paused by the window. Ian and Cara were outside, loading their luggage into the trunk of their own taxi. Or, more precisely, loading Ian's luggage; Cara seemed to have all of her gear in a single canvas backpack. Ian had three large suitcases and a trunk.

"Dan? You ready?"

Amy stood at the door.

"Yeah." Dan brushed his hair from his face. "You?"

Amy nodded. "Suitcase is in the hall."

They stood facing each other, the gap filling with an awkward silence.

"You'll be careful, right?" said Amy. "I mean, no stupid heroics."

"And the same goes for you. Leave the charming to Jonah and the heavy lifting to Ham."

"What does that leave me?"

"Be the brains of the outfit. Beat Nathaniel."

Amy smiled. "Got it." She stepped back and ruffled his hair.

"Hey!" Dan swatted her away.

"What! You're taller than me now—soon I won't be able to reach!"

They stood side by side. Not so different, as siblings could be. And yes, he was taller now. Dan grinned. "I'm not your little brother anymore."

Amy laughed. "Yes, you are. And you always will be."

He wanted to tell her he loved her and that she needed to take care. That she was more important than all the Cahills past and present put together and multiplied by a hundred. That she'd never be like Grace, that she'd be *better*.

But another taxi rolled up and honked its horn. Dan picked up his backpack and, with one last look at his sister, walked out the door.

CHAPTER 10

Attleboro, Massachusetts

Nathaniel Hartford gazed admiringly at the model of the *Wright Flyer*. It was perfect in every detail, replicating the first-ever truly modern airplane in precious metals. The struts were platinum wire, the frame gold, and the wings beaten silver. The model stood upon a pedestal carved from an unearthly piece of rock.

He turned it around, letting the morning sun that slipped through the windows of the Cahill study strike and warm every surface.

He loved technology and was grateful to have been born into the most technologically advanced age of mankind. How many thousands of years had people struggled with stone? Then metal and animal power? *Now look at us.*

To think they'd come from the *Wright Flyer* to space travel within a single lifetime. Hence the pedestal, a rock from the moon itself.

He looked about the study with satisfaction. All

traces of the Cahill children and that Kabra boy had been removed and it was now entirely *his*.

Yet Grace still lingered. He could not remove her from the mansion without dismantling every brick. Her ghost seemed to haunt each room, each corridor. Wherever Nathaniel turned, there she was. At the desk. By the window. Reading in the library.

"Isn't this how it should have been, Grace?" Nathaniel asked the silence. "Haven't I proven I was worthy to lead the family?"

There was no answer, but Nathaniel could feel her scorn.

"The Cahill legacy," Nathaniel sneered. "That's all that mattered to you, wasn't it? That the family would go on. And on. And on. Pulling the strings, guiding the fate of the world. And the world turned out so well, didn't it?"

Nathaniel rested his fists on the desk. Was this the very desk Grace had sat at when she'd signed the order for his death? He was sure it was. "You know what they say about absolute power? That it corrupts absolutely. You were the finest example of that. A vindictive, bitter tyrant, quite willing to destroy the lives of anyone who crossed her. Never considering others might be better suited. Or that the Cahills have had their day."

He smiled to himself. "It's time to deal with your legacy once and for all."

Nathaniel paused at a piece of fused glass. He'd collected it from what had been the city of Hiroshima. It was fascinating how many technological leaps were made during periods of conflict. What was it that tied creativity to the urge to destroy?

If only I had ten years more. Even just another five. What things I might see.

He returned to the table, *his* table.

Things were proceeding almost perfectly. Almost.

Alek Spasky was becoming a problem. No matter, once this business was over, Alek would have no need of him, and Nathaniel would have no need of Alek.

Never trust a traitor, Alek. A spy should know that.

The phone rang.

Nathaniel hit the speaker button. "Yes?"

"We have another sighting of Dan Cahill, sir."

It was one of the surveillance teams he'd recruited. "Put it up on the screen."

Dan Cahill stood, poised at the immigration desk at the French-German border. He was smiling awkwardly at the immigration officer, who was reaching to inspect his passport.

Facial recognition technology was getting better and better. Accuracy was over 99.9% with the software one of his companies had developed. But the last two days had registered false alarms all over the world. That could only mean one thing. Someone had sabotaged his system. He had software engineers trying to fix it, but whoever had done it was good, better than his own people.

So he'd seen Dan in Warsaw, in Delhi, in Mexico City. He needed the Cahill boy, so men had been sent to each location.

And now this.

What was he doing in Germany? Nathaniel hadn't been there in decades.

He paused. Could it be . . . ? He shivered, then a dark anger pulsed at the back of his head.

The Cahill children were not to be underestimated. If Dan was in Germany, he was there because *something* had brought him there.

The Black Forest facility.

Not this time, Grace.

He reached for his phone. There were three numbers on his speed dial. He pressed the top one.

"Melinda? It's Nathaniel. Are you still in Paris? Good. I need you on the first plane to Germany." Nathaniel smiled. "I have a little job for you. . . ."

CHAPTER 11

Kiev, Ukraine

"I still can't believe we're doing this," said Cara as she watched Ian gather his luggage off the carousel. "You really think we can persuade Alek Spasky to just spill the beans?"

Ian dropped the third suitcase onto the luggage cart. "If not him, then the woman he's going to see. You heard him. This 'Natalia' means a lot to him, and something's changed between him and Nathaniel. Something we can use to our advantage."

They'd reached Ukraine's largest international airport, Boryspil, a day behind Alek Spasky. There were three suitcases on the cart already and Ian was struggling with the fourth, a grand trunk that could be turned into a rowboat if necessary.

He did not believe in traveling light.

"Need a hand?" Cara asked. Her entire gear had folded up into her backpack. That included her laptop, spare coat, and a solar-powered recharger.

"Do you mind? Just grab the other end and lift on the count of three."

On the count of three they got the trunk onto the luggage cart. Cara didn't like the way the wheels buckled. "What have you got in there?"

"A few essential toiletries. This is Ukraine, you know. Apart from a rather wonderful supply of caviar, they do lack a few of the . . . luxuries one is accustomed to. And man cannot live off caviar alone."

"Though you've tried, right?"

"Second year of boarding school. Honestly, the food they served us would have made a polar bear sick. Fortunately, I had a distant aunt who knew a man in the Ukrainian navy who—"

"Enough, Ian." Cara helped steer the cart through customs. "So where do we go from here?"

"I've contacted an old family friend of ours, Uncle Dmitry," said Ian. "I've asked him to help us out."

"You've an uncle out here?"

"Not a blood relative, but during the collapse of the Soviet Union, my father realized there were quite a few business opportunities to be had. How do you think we bought our Caribbean island? He needed a local willing to, well, go off-piste when necessary. Dmitry Melnikov was a private investigator who helped smooth out some business transactions. I called him to keep an eye out for our Mr. Spasky."

They steered the cart out into the main hall.

"Ian!" A big man barged through the crowd and lifted Ian off his feet in a bear hug. He kissed Ian, now blushing, once on each cheek. "My little prince! Ah, not so little anymore, eh?"

Ian wiped his cheeks. "Hello, Uncle Dmitry. It has been a long time. This is my . . . friend Cara."

Dmitry waggled his bushy eyebrows. "So the little prince has a little princess now?"

Cara held out her hand. "Hello, Mr. Melnikov."

Dmitry brushed it aside and embraced her, too. "Who is this Mr. Melnikov? I am your Uncle Dmitry!"

He led them to a car outside. A small car. A *really* small car.

It was an East German Trabant. One window was cracked, another taped, and the doors were lined with orange rust. It couldn't be more than four feet high, and not much longer. Cara walked around it. How were three adults expected to fit in? "Who's this for? Munchkins?"

"What happened to the Mercedes?" asked Ian.

Dmitry took a screwdriver to the trunk to open it. "First wife took beautiful car." The trunk creaked open. "Second wife took house. Third took dacha. And fourth took Lenin."

"Lenin?"

Dmitry sighed. "My dog. I miss Lenin."

"Maybe we should take a taxi. . . ." Ian waved at a metered SUV on the corner.

Dmitry grabbed his arm and forced it down. "Taxi? Taxi drivers are nothing but thieves! There is plenty of room! We will put your box on the roof!"

"Uncle Dmitry," started Ian. "That 'box' as you call it is a limited edition Louis Vuitton Excelsior cruising trunk. It does *not* go on the roof."

Ian might as well have been talking to the wind. Dmitry hauled it up to the top of his Trabant. It was bound tightly with blue nylon rope and the ends threaded through the open windows. Dmitry squeezed in, lit a cigar, and turned the ignition.

The engine coughed to life.

Dmitry grinned as he patted the dashboard. "Not failed yet!"

Dmitry took them to a dull, gray apartment tower on the outskirts of Kiev, one among a long avenue of identical drab towers. The elevator didn't work and, judging by the rust, hadn't since the fall of the Berlin Wall. Dmitry balanced Ian's trunk on his shoulders. "Only ten floors!"

The corridor lights flickered irregularly and the walls were decorated with graffiti. A stray cat picked at an old box of rice forgotten on the landing.

Ian put his handkerchief to his face. "Charming."

The cat hissed as they passed by.

The apartment walls were bare concrete slabs that had been pasted over with thin wallpaper; the floors were covered with even thinner carpet. Great patches had worn through, revealing the slab underneath. An armchair faced an old cathode-ray television set, and there were loose cables strung from the hi-fi to a clutter of speakers balanced on shelves in the corners. A faded red curtain separated the main living room from the small kitchenette.

"Welcome, welcome!" Dmitry declared, dropping the trunk with a frame-cracking thud. He walked up to a small cage by the window. Two mice appeared from the piles of paper and sniffed the bars as he dropped in some cheese. *"Zdravstvuitye*, Mickey! *Privyet*, Jerry!"

"What's this?" Ian stopped by the dining table.

Notes, photographs, maps, and documents covered the warped wooden top. Cara joined him and picked up the nearest photograph.

And looked into the cold gaze of Alek Spasky.

"When was this taken?" she asked, unable to control a shiver.

Dmitry filled up a kettle and set it on the electric cooktop. "Last night. Your friend is here in Kiev."

Cara met Ian's frowning gaze. Yes, she knew exactly what he was feeling. Worried to the extreme.

"We need to know what Alek is up to. Give us a lead?" Ian said.

Dmitry slapped his back. "The little prince is a warrior—now, that I like! I have something that may help. No prince goes into battle without a sword, eh?"

While Dmitry started rummaging under the sofa, the two of them looked through the pile of information the private eye had gathered for them. Dmitry might have lived in chaos, but his skills at information gathering were as focused as a laser beam.

Ian picked up a list of old flights. "That's strange. Alek comes here every year. Has done . . . for a long time."

Cara checked. The dates went back decades. "You think this is something to do with Nathaniel?"

"No. Alek had nothing to do with the Cahills until recently. So this is either KGB work, or it's personal."

"Alek Spasky was top man with KGB. You need to be very careful." Dmitry dragged out a suitcase from under the sofa. It was covered in painted flowers. Dmitry smiled shyly. "My mother's."

Inside were guns. Lots of guns.

Ian's eyebrows rose. "Your mother lives in a tough neighborhood? Like downtown Baghdad?"

Dmitry drew one out of its wrapping. "German made. The best. Heckler and Koch P30, 9mm. Only 740 grams. Here, you try." He slid over a box of bullets. "Just shoot out the window. Neighbor is deaf."

"Er . . . no, thanks."

"What you want? I have Beretta. Or a nice Walther PPK, same as your James Bond! No crease in jacket."

Cara noticed Ian's gaze pause on the small pistol. No doubt the creasing of his jacket was a major concern for Ian. But he shook his head and handed the pistol back. "I'm British, Dmitry. We try not to use guns."

"Then what you use?"

"Usually a stern word or disapproving look does the job."

Dmitry's cell phone buzzed, and he left Cara and Ian to inspect the suitcase of guns.

"If we come face-to-face with Alek, a gun will make no difference," said Ian.

"Why not?"

"Because we will lose, Cara." Ian put the pistol back and closed the lid. "How much experience do you have shooting people?"

"None. Thank goodness."

Dmitry finished his conversation and joined them. "We must go. My brother has been keeping a watch on Alek. He has left his hotel and taken a car north on the P02 road. We must follow."

"The P02?" asked Ian. "Where does it go?"

"To Pripyat," said Dmitry, grimly. "The city of ghosts."

CHAPTER 12

Dmitry drove. He brought a pistol for himself and a Geiger counter. "Just to be sure," he said. "With Chernobyl, you can never be too careful."

Cara knew Dmitry had every reason to be cautious. She'd read up on the 1986 nuclear disaster on the flight over. Faulty design had led to one of the reactors overheating. Normally, the heat was absorbed by cooling water flowing through the system, but the water had turned to steam and caused a pressure buildup within the reactor. Then, like a balloon, it had exploded, hurling radioactive material into the atmosphere. A few seconds later a second explosion threw more radioactive material out.

The immediate death toll hadn't been high. Two people were killed in the initial explosion, then more than thirty rescue workers and other staff died of radiation poisoning over the next few months. There had almost been a much bigger explosion, but three engineers had volunteered to wade into the radioactive cooling water and drain it to prevent another steam explosion when waste began burning through the reactor floor, down into the pools below.

Cara wondered what they must have felt, knowing they were going to their deaths.

But the effects of the explosion were still being felt today. Estimates varied, but the radiation had left a trail of cancer around the globe.

"Pripyat a bad place," Dmitry said as they joined the P02 north. "City built next to Chernobyl for housing the workers. When reactor explode, entire city becomes contaminated. They evacuate all people. Now no one live there. We go, but can only stay a few hours before risk of contamination, *da*?"

Cara knew the story, too, but there was nothing like actually approaching the infamous city. "The radioactive material has a half-life of hundreds of thousands of years. Pripyat will remain empty for another twenty thousand at least before it's safe to be inhabited again," she told Ian. "It's safe-ish for a day, but not much longer."

"How far is it?" asked Ian, sitting next to her in the back.

"Two hours," said Dmitry.

"And why does Alek go there?"

Dmitry shrugged. "Every year he make same trip. There and back in one day. He not stay long."

The Trabant fought over the humps and potholes on the road. They stopped for a refill halfway, and for a simple packet of sandwiches.

"You have money, little prince?" asked Dmitry.

Ian opened up his wallet and handed over the Ukrainian hryvnia.

Cara saw the way Dmitry stared at the cash. He was hungry, and those sandwiches weren't going to fill him up. While Dmitry went off to pay for the gasoline, Cara nudged Ian. "Dmitry's not doing this for free, you know."

"I realize that," said Ian. "But he knows he'll be well paid once Nathaniel is defeated and I can access the family funds."

"So you're counting on his goodwill until then?"

Ian grinned, and that flash of teeth and look in his eyes made Cara . . . well, feel something about him. "Don't worry, this is Uncle Dmitry we're talking about. He's family!"

Dmitry waved a paper bag. "Who want pickled cabbage sandwich?"

Cara smiled and took hers. She watched Ian and Dmitry laugh about past adventures. Maybe Ian was right about Dmitry. But she wasn't so sure. Maybe he was family, but with Ian, that wasn't saying much.

The city came into view sooner than Cara would have liked.

Eerie, that was the word that sprang to Cara's mind.

The buildings were all in the ugly Soviet Bloc style: drab, monolithic, identical. They had fallen into disrepair. Windows were opaque with dust.

Piles of leaves and trash gathered in the doorways and narrow alleyways. The foliage ran rampant; roots broke up the paving and the roads. Bushes had consumed some of the abandoned cars. Everything was the color of rust. The vehicles, the lampposts, the railings, the gates and bus shelters. The parks were a wilderness now, the grass six feet high and thick with weeds. Ivy wrapped around the climbing frames and the swings. The children's animal rockers were weathered, the paint patchy, making them look as if they had a skin disease. They passed a square with a once-proud statue of a heroic worker. Now the man's face was pitted, cracked, and stained. Moss covered his lower body, transforming him into a strange mutant, half man and half vegetation.

A bus drove by, slowly, filled with tourists taking photos.

Dmitry parked and dialed his cell. The conversation was quick. He scowled. "Alek has stopped. My brother will not follow any farther."

Ian held on to the Geiger counter. "Where is he?"

"Another kilometer and a half along this road. At the city graveyard." Dmitry held out his weapon. "Are you sure you don't want?"

"Not the sort of place I'd take a woman on a date," said Ian. "A graveyard in an abandoned city."

Cara nodded. "At least you know you'll be alone."

Ian paused. "I'm having second thoughts about

this. Trailing Alek Spasky through a graveyard just seems . . . highly ominous?"

Cara took his hand. "Come on, Ian."

They crept along, keeping Alek just in sight. The graveyard was huge and rambling, with bushes and trees. The gravestones were large, the statues old and vine-woven.

"Where do you think he's going?" Cara asked.

"Somewhere isolated, with two freshly dug graves," said Ian.

"If he was planning to kill us why does he have flowers?"

"Russian sense of humor?"

"Wait. He stopped." Cara pulled Ian down behind a gravestone.

Ian peered around the side. "I don't see anyone else."

Where was Natalia? The flowers must be for her, yet there was no one in sight.

It was hard to imagine a lonelier place. Not even the wind disturbed the somber silence, and if there were any birds, they were minding their own business.

Ian hated graveyards. Especially ones with KGB assassins in them.

He must be insane, being this close to Alek Spasky. They should have stayed farther back. Way farther back. Like, back in London.

Ian had never really taken a good look at Alek. Now he could, and saw a middle-aged man, hair short-cropped with plenty of gray in it. The face was hard, bare of any fat or softness, a classic Russian face made up of high cheekbones and brooding brow. His mouth was wide, but his lips thin. It was tough to imagine a mouth like that smiling, or laughing.

Alek paused and looked around.

Ian held his breath, daring not to move. Cara squeezed his hand.

Alek's eyes narrowed.

Ian felt his heart hammering against his ribs. He was sweating—a bead of moisture dribbled down his temple, but he didn't dare move to brush it away. The slightest action might catch Alek's attention.

Alek reached into his coat . . .

How far would they get if they ran now?

Not far enough.

. . . and drew out a handkerchief.

"Phew," whispered Cara.

Pollen tickled Ian's nostrils. It was late spring and everything was blooming. He held his hand-kerchief to his nose. Oh, no—he really needed to sneeze. . . .

Cara pinched his nostrils together. "One sniff out of you and we'll have Alek skewering us with one of his darts."

"Eep" was as much as Ian could manage.

They watched Alek clear weeds and dead leaves off a grave. He was kneeling and, from here, it looked as if he was talking. Then he brushed his hands and arranged the fresh flowers on top of the grave.

Who was buried there?

It couldn't be his sister; Irina was buried in Moscow.

Ian frowned. As far as he knew there were no Spasky connections in Ukraine.

"He's leaving," whispered Cara.

Ian glanced over the stone slab. "And he's left the flowers."

Alek was back on the path. He looked back at the grave once, and briefly. As if saying good-bye. Then he straightened himself and left.

"Should we follow him?" Cara was already on her feet.

"No." Ian peered over to the grave and the flowers. "I want to see who's buried there."

"But we'll lose Alek."

"And somehow I feel his and our paths will cross again, whether we like it or not." Ian began walking. "We need to check this out, Cara."

The roses were deep red and bound with a black ribbon. Green moss clung to the granite gravestone, and it was weathered and patchy with stains.

Ian froze as he read the name. "Of course."

" 'Doctor Natalia Ivanova Spasky. Beloved wife.' " Cara rubbed the moss off the dates. " 'Born 1st July 1961. Died 12th July 1986. Age 25.' His wife?"

"Yes, she must be," said Ian. "She died a few months after the Chernobyl incident. That seems too much of a coincidence. She was very young to have a doctorate. She must have been bright." He knew plenty of Ekats who were professors in their early and midtwenties, straight As all the way since kindergarten. "I wonder . . ."

"He must have loved her so much." Cara stared at the grave. "Still giving her flowers, thirty years later."

Ian faced the worn gravestone. "We need to find out about Natalia Spasky."

CHAPTER 13

Stuttgart, Germany

"Hi, Stuttgart. Bye, Stuttgart," said Dan, shifting in his seat, trying to find some position that worked. His backside was numb and his legs were cramping. He bunched up his jacket as a pillow and wedged it under his neck and against the side of the seat.

And sat, eyes open, sleep a long, long way away.

Nellie and Sammy snored. Sammy was slumped over the armrest and Nellie was using his shoulder for her pillow. They were even holding hands.

Dan sighed. He stared out the train window.

Trees lined the railway, allowing only fleeting glimpses of town or village lights as the train sped by. He'd heard it stop, somewhere, and there'd been voices and movement on the platform as half-awake passengers climbed off.

By now, the train was partially empty. Sammy snorted and swapped sides. He fell against Dan, forcing him harder against the wall.

"That's it." Dan pushed Sammy off. "I've had it."

He grabbed Nellie's map and guidebook. The dining car was open, and lit. He'd pick up a snack and a drink and read in there. With any luck he'd get really tired, then try to put his head down for the few hours remaining before they reached their destination.

He didn't bother with his new hiking boots—they chafed and he already had a blister on each heel. The thick socks would work fine as slippers.

There was something about trains. The pace. Trains didn't feel like rushing.

Maybe that's why Amy sent me on this trip.

A man edged along the narrow passageway, yawning. He smiled at Dan as he went past. Another insomniac traveler.

Dan entered the dining car. The clock said 4 A.M., and the counter was closed. He had his choice of a trio of vending machines humming along the wall. Dan chucked in a handful of euros and got himself an orange juice and a doughnut.

There was just one other guy here. A businessman, deep in a big novel, with a cup of tea steaming on the table next to him. He glanced up as Dan came in, then went back to his book.

Dan chewed on his doughnut and spread out the map carefully. Nellie would have some choice words if he ended up getting sugar all over it.

Now, where was the Black Forest? Way down there. He traced the train track down from Stuttgart, checking the names of the towns and other locations. They were just coming up to another crossing over the Rhine River soon; the train track had run alongside it for most of the journey.

"*Wo gehst du hin?*"

Dan looked up and met the gaze of the business-man. He had his reading glasses perched on the tip of his nose as he looked down at Dan's map.

"I'm sorry, er, I . . . *ich verstehe Sie nicht*?"

"Ah! You are English?"

"American."

"American! *Gut!*" He smiled and tucked away his novel. "You go to Stuttgart?"

Dan shook his head. "We're just stopping there, then going on."

The businessman looked him up and down. "Ah! Backpacking, *ja*? Many students in Germany. Beautiful country. Many *Jugendherbergen* in Germany! How you say . . . young hostels?"

"Youth hostels?"

"*Ja!*" He licked his lips, then tried out the words. "Youth hostels."

The guy seemed to want to test out his English, and Dan wasn't going to sleep anytime soon. He offered him a seat and looked over the map. "We're going camping here."

"Schwarzwald? How you say . . . Black Forest? Very beautiful!"

The last thing Dan wanted was to get trapped with a fellow passenger. He smiled and stood. "I'm going to try to get some sleep."

The businessman grabbed his wrist. "Please stay, I insist."

The German accent was gone. Instead, the guy spoke in clear, cold English.

The far door opened.

And Melinda Toth entered.

CHAPTER 14

Melinda smiled at him. Beside her was a second henchman, the guy Dan had passed in the corridor earlier. He gently closed the door behind him.

"Your grandfather's been looking for you, Dan," said Melinda. "He's got something rather *special* planned."

That sounded all sorts of bad.

Dan's blood chilled. He wrestled with the fear that was building up in his chest, threatening to rob him of his wits, threatening to freeze his mind and body.

The fake German businessman twisted Dan's wrists sharply and shoved him to the floor in front of Melinda.

She glanced over her shoulder to the second man. "Find Dan's compartment. Make sure the other two are locked in." She smiled at Dan. "We don't want any interruptions, do we?"

Dan's mind raced. He had two options: fight or flight. He was outnumbered and outgunned. Melinda was bad enough, and her two goons looked like they knew what they were doing. Given Nathaniel's resources and Melinda's contacts, he'd guess they were ex-Special Forces, a cut above mere muscle. No way was he going to win a straight fight and no way was he going to talk his way out of it. So that left only one option.

Surprise.

He drooped. He sank his head down, let his shoulders fall. He needed them to believe he was beaten; it might make them less wary. It wasn't much of a chance, but it was all he had. Dan rubbed his wrist. "How did you find me?"

"You can't hide from technology, Dan." Melinda motioned with her finger. "Get up, boy."

Dan did. Fast.

He bowled into her, using her as a mat as he rolled over her and onto his feet. The fake German launched himself at Dan.

Dan went for the door, then swung it open, hard.

Straight into the guy's face.

Dan hopped over the stunned man and ran.

She'd sent her other henchman back down the train, so the only way was forward. He needed to find a way to double back and get to Nellie and Sammy, but that meant—

The lightbulb exploded as a bullet hit it. Glass sprinkled down on Dan as he dove for the other door.

"No!" yelled Melinda. "We need him alive!"

That's good to know.

Dan ran through the next car. He tested the door handles into their compartment, but they were locked. He could beat on them for help, but he knew the type of men Melinda had brought with her. He wasn't going to risk innocent lives like that. There had to be another way.

He pushed on into the next car, the luggage part of the train. Twenty or so bikes were neatly slotted into their stands, and there were backpacks labeled and shoved onto shelves.

Dan pulled an aluminum pump off a bike and wedged it into the door. *That will buy me another thirty seconds.*

He tested the side door, but no luck. Locked.

He had to get back to the others. But there was only one way to do that. He'd have to get back to his car by walking along the roof.

Of a high-speed train. In the middle of the night.

Dan grimaced. *Why does it always happen to me?*

He braced himself against the rack and slammed his socked feet into the center of the window. The pane reverberated but held.

Teeth gritted, he repeated it again and again, beating his heels into the glass.

"Come on . . ."

Over the din of the rattling wheels he heard a noise at the car door.

A crack blossomed in the glass under his feet. Air hummed through it, sending the curtains flapping wildly.

The door handle turned and shook as someone outside slammed against it.

"Don't make it hard on yourself, Dan!" shouted Melinda. "Open up!"

Dan looped both hands on the rack and raised his feet. Where was Ham when you needed him? He'd have broken the glass just by staring at it.

"Open up, Dan!"

Dan roared as he slammed both feet into the window.

It exploded and the car instantly filled with screaming air.

"Don't be stupid!" Melinda must have guessed what he was planning.

To get out the only way he could.

The trees whipped by, long twigs laden with leaves lashed at the train, and the wind's howl joined the noise of engine and steel wheels to create a deafening roar.

Yeah, this is stupid to the extreme.

Dan grinned—he couldn't help himself. *Stupid in a long line of stupid.*

He kicked out the bigger shard still stuck in the frame and then, hooking his fingers along the upper edge, hopped up onto the frame.

The wind stung his eyes, making it impossible to see what was up ahead. All he needed was a big branch to smash him off.

He slid one hand up the smooth, sooty outer

surface of the car. His fingers searched for something to latch on to.

The car tilted as it jerked around a corner and Dan winced, legs shaking to keep balance on the thin frame. There. He felt along a slot. A vent? He squeezed his fingers into the gap and curled them around a narrow, sharp opening.

The doorframe cracked as Melinda, or more likely one of her henchmen, crashed against the car door. One more hit and it would be nothing but splinters.

It was now or never.

Dan jammed his other hand into the vent and hauled himself up, springing halfway out the window.

The door crashed open.

"Quick! Grab him!" yelled Melinda.

A chunky hand grabbed Dan's left foot, but he lashed out with his right and there was a satisfying, fleshy thump, the kind you might get when a foot meets a face. The man's grip slipped and Dan hauled himself fully out the window.

This wasn't just stupid. This was *crazy* stupid.

The wind pulled and pushed him as if trying to rip him off the train. Dan had to slide himself upward, pressed flat against the metal surface of the car until it leveled out at the top. He slowly got to his feet, poised in a crouch to cut down the wind resistance. Even then he could barely stop from toppling over.

The forest was a blur and the moon shone on the train, lighting a shiny silver path on the roof. The engine ahead roared like an angry dragon.

Now what? Forward or back?

The choice was made for him as Melinda rose up onto the roof behind him. She'd gone out between the cars and climbed up.

Dan knew what was going to happen. If she was behind him, then she'd have sent one of her minions to do the same . . . from the front.

Dan ran. A head appeared in the gap ahead, and he picked up the pace, ignoring the horrific way the train juddered on the tracks, and leaped across to the next car.

"Dan!" shouted Melinda. "There's no way off this train!"

There was real fear in her voice, and she was shuffling along, arms outstretched like a tightrope walker.

She was right. If he got into any car, they'd get him. All he was doing was dragging it out. But Dan wasn't going to just raise his hands and give up.

"Got you!"

A hand clamped down on Dan's shoulder and he kicked out instinctively.

His heel rammed into the man's shin and the man buckled. Dan twisted sharply, slamming both fists down on the man's forearm to break the grip.

The train jerked sideways as it swapped tracks.

Dan fought to stay upright, managing to keep on his feet and on the train roof, barely.

The minion wasn't so lucky. Big, meaty, and not at all quick or nimble, he yelled as he toppled backward and disappeared into a thicket of trees.

Melinda cursed and was edging closer. She drew something out of her jacket pocket—a short metal stub that, with a flick, sprang into a foot-long steel baton.

"Nathaniel wants you alive," she snarled. "But that doesn't stop me from breaking a few bones."

Dan tugged off his jacket and wrapped it around his left arm.

Melinda smirked. "Where'd you learn that? From YouTube?"

Dan blushed. How did she know?

Melinda moved more confidently now, sliding one foot ahead and keeping her eyes on Dan. He had to shuffle backward, not daring to look where he was going in case she attacked.

And then she did.

Dan raised his arm to ward off the hit, but it was a feint; Melinda flipped the weapon and brought it slamming into the side of Dan's knee. He yelled, but didn't fall. The next blow was a sharp jab in the gut before a flick into his jaw.

It had only been seconds and Dan was reeling. He punched out, but all that got him was a bruised wrist as Melinda snapped the baton across it.

"Had enough?" she taunted.

There was no overconfidence, just an assurance she was in charge, and Dan knew it.

He needed to get past that stick of hers.

So Dan charged.

Melinda brought both elbows into the back of his neck as Dan rammed her off her feet. They slammed into the hard steel and Melinda gasped. They slid across the roof, gravity pulling them down the curved slope toward the edge. Melinda cried out, then caught her foot on the ridge, holding them both on the top of the speeding train, but only just.

Dan rammed his fist into her, but Melinda hooked a leg around his neck and trapped his arm between hers. She twisted, and it felt as if Dan's arm was about to be ripped out of his shoulder socket.

Dan sank his teeth into one of her calves and Melinda snarled. He tugged himself free and stumbled back to his feet.

"Biting? Seriously?" Melinda limped to her feet. "What's next? Hair pulling?"

Dan spat out a few threads of nylon. He had to get away.

A black winding line bisected the track ahead of them. Dan's photographic memory flashed up an image he'd glimpsed at the train station.

The train dipped as the front cars ran onto a bridge.

We're crossing the Rhine River.

"Don't be stupid!" yelled Melinda.

Dan ran forward. The iron bridge was a single

span, fifty or so feet over the river itself. The fall might kill him, but it seemed better than being handed over to the Outcast.

The timing had to be perfect. Too soon, and he'd break himself against the steel girders of the bridge arch and too slow, he'd miss the river entirely. So it had to be . . .

Now!

"Dan!" Melinda screamed as he launched himself off the train.

Dan spun through the air. It was like falling forever. Time slowed, and he was staring at trees and stars and train and rushing water, all tumbling around and around. He gasped for air, pushing against the panic that seized his lungs. How far? How far? There were rocks and girders and the black roaring river and its white rapids rushing up fast to hit him and—

He crashed helter-skelter into the water. Hard.

Down and down he sank, dragged by the tumultuous rapids. He was battered and shoved. It felt as if he was being grabbed, held under, despite how hard he beat his arms and legs. The river had him and didn't want to let go. He crashed into and bounced off a submerged rock, hitting it with his shoulder.

Dan tumbled into the swirl; he was dragged and shoved, pummeled by the hard, chaotic current. He flailed and kicked, trying to get right-side up. He broke the surface and gasped.

He glimpsed a second figure—a slash of red in the air—then a splash as Melinda hit the water.

He shivered but struck out toward the bank. It was tantalizingly close, but the river still wanted him.

Drooping fronds brushed the water's surface and Dan stretched up to grab them. They bent, arcing low to the river, but held.

"Help me!" Melinda screamed.

Dan spun to see Melinda sweep by. Their eyes met; he would never forget the look of fear, lit by the heartless moonlight, before Melinda was carried away. She rolled in the rapids and disappeared under.

Dan ached as he hung on to the fronds. He shivered but forced himself to crawl along until his feet touched the pebbly river bottom. Then he stumbled up the riverbank and collapsed.

He felt as if he'd gone ten rounds with Mike Tyson. Every part of him had been pummeled until he was one huge world of pain.

The sound of a car engine made him raise his head. Headlights slipped out across the river's surface as a hulking SUV pushed itself out through the wall of trees along the river's edge.

"Help . . ." Dan muttered, his lungs too tired to raise his voice beyond a whisper.

The car stopped, its engine rumbled idly. The passenger door opened and Dan, face still in the dirt, glimpsed a pair of well-polished shoes step out.

"He's alive, sir."

"Get him up."

Hands roughly hoisted Dan to his feet. He peered into the blinding headlights. It hurt to look, but then everything hurt right now.

There were two big men who couldn't have been more "bodyguard" if they'd worn red T-shirts that said, CALL ME MR. BODYGUARD. They stood on either side of a much frailer figure, hand on a walking stick.

Nathaniel Hartford paused to look up at the bridge so very high above them. "I am most impressed. The fall itself would kill the average man."

Dan tugged, but he was held firm. He glared at Nathaniel. "Out for some late-night fishing?"

Nathaniel nodded to the man holding him. "Please, make him shut up."

Dan winced as the needle jabbed his neck. Then a weight, piles of wet sand, pressed down over him and he sank and sank. . . .

CHAPTER 15

Kiev, Ukraine

Ian sat up front in the Trabant, his knees somewhere up by his chin. Cara was squashed in the back, peering out the window.

They were back in Kiev. Dmitry's car had decided to have a rest for no mechanical reason at all, so the drive had taken twice as long as expected. Ian had watched Dmitry hit the engine with a wrench, a hammer, and finally his boot, and he'd also learned a few new Russian curses.

Now they were watching Dmitry and a security guard, both men standing outside a grim-looking squat government building, having a friendly chat.

Eventually, Dmitry shook hands and handed over a small paper bag. The man checked its contents, nodded, and wandered off. Dmitry scurried back to the car, grinning. "All good. You have one hour."

Ian frowned. "For five hundred euros? I thought we agreed a whole afternoon."

Dmitry tapped the side of his nose. "One hour to

see KGB files, best I could do, little prince. All very secret."

Secret? Ian almost laughed. The security was ridiculous. The cameras weren't even connected to power. Only the first-floor windows had any bars on them, and the guard at the front looked like Santa's bigger, older, more-bearded brother.

"Now, this is old school," said Ian as he slid the microfiche into the reader. "Keep an eye on the door."

Ian had a pile of the transparent sheets of film, all in date order and covering a month before the nuclear disaster and five months after.

The sheets contained pages reduced to a fraction of their original size, so a single sheet could hold hundreds of pages of information. Back before the days of computing, this had been the best way to store data.

The reader was really just a backlit magnifying glass, the size of an old-style cathode-ray TV, and Ian had to turn the focus to sharpen the image.

He wasn't sure what he was looking for as he scanned through the pages. Soviet-era news wasn't exactly reliable, so governmental files were their best bet, but Ian guessed there were plenty of people in power who'd not be pleased with him and Cara digging through the Chernobyl disaster. Some of them might even call it "spying," and there were severe penalties for that.

"Do they still have gulags here?" Ian asked. He didn't fancy a few decades in a Ukrainian prison.

"What?"

"Sorry. Just thinking out loud." Then he stopped. "Here we go. The death certificates following the Chernobyl disaster."

"Well?"

"One of them's for Natalia."

"What's it say?"

" 'Acute radiation poisoning.' " Ian spotted a note tagged on the corner referring to another file. He flipped the reader open and searched the pile until he found it. "There's more about Natalia on this."

Ian read the document, testing his fluency reading Russian Cyrillic. "Star of Moscow University's physics department. Top honors throughout. Then a stint at MIT through a private, unknown sponsor. MIT? Now, that was just up the road from—"

"Grace's mansion," said Cara.

"You thinking what I'm thinking?"

"Natalia was an Ekat? Yes, I am," said Cara. "This looks like exactly the sort of thing Grace would have pulled. She spots a talent within the family and nurtures it. Geopolitics be damned." She leaned over to have a better look at the file. "Then what?"

"Natalia returns to the USSR but lands herself a lowly teaching assistant job. The government at the time would have seen her as spoiled goods, someone tainted by Western ideology. She was probably lucky to be teaching at all. Then, a day after the

Chernobyl meltdown, she ferries herself off to Ukraine and offers her services directly to the team. Whoever's in charge recognizes her value, and in she goes. She was part of the team of engineers who sacrificed themselves to open up the cooling water drains that prevented a second series of explosions. They knew they were going to their deaths, but that didn't stop them."

Cara looked thoughtful. "Not many people on the planet would have the courage to do that."

Ian had to agree. He'd faced gunmen and killers, but that was courage of the moment, a rush of adrenaline and the urge to protect his friends from danger. Allowing yourself to die by radiation poisoning was a whole different level of bravery.

"Natalia Spasky must have been a very special woman," said Cara. "Any mention of Alek?"

"No," replied Ian. "But I'm not surprised. He was well in with the KGB by that point. Her relationship with him would have broken all sorts of security rules." He paused and increased the magnification. "Wait a minute. There's a handwritten note. It's referring to another report. Is there a report twenty-seven in the drawer?"

Cara searched and a moment later handed him a folder. "Twenty-seven."

The papers had yellowed with age and there were plenty of them, a bundle over an inch thick. Ian scanned the first few pages, the report summary. "It's an investigation into the theft of nuclear materials from the reactor. It seems they were being sold on the black market."

"Wow. That's really very bad news."

"Yes. The USSR was on its last legs and my father said it was a boom time for arms smugglers. As the Soviet Union collapsed, there were generals selling off tanks, ships were disappearing from docks, and even the odd submarine was on the market. Quality-grade plutonium would have fetched millions on the black market from any rogue state wanting to build its own bomb." He gasped. "It can't be . . ."

"Ian?"

Ian rubbed his eyes and reread the document, not trusting his translation. He had to be wrong. . . .

But the words were the same. And horrifying in their magnitude.

"This report . . ." He hesitated, guts tightening with the implications of the document. "It says the disaster was no accident. It was sabotage!"

Cara stared. "Sabotage? That's insane!"

Ian forced himself to continue. "Done to cover up the missing plutonium. It talks about an arms smuggler, an American with extensive Russian contacts." Ian flicked through the folder. "The KGB managed to get a photograph of him while he was here in Ukraine, days after the disaster. Then he vanished." Ian inspected a sheaf of photographs—and froze. "No."

It was blurry, a picture snatched in secret of a

man getting into a car. He had glasses on and the collar to his jacket turned up. "This is bad, Cara."

Cara peered over his shoulder at the enlarged image. She gasped as she recognized him.

It was Nathaniel Hartford.

CHAPTER 16

"Time's ticking, Ian. I think we've got enough," said Cara as she gazed over Dmitry's apartment.

Every patch of floor was covered with reports and sheets of microfiche they'd taken from the KGB office.

They'd been working all evening, searching through the papers and scanning the microfiches with magnifying glasses.

But the information was gold dust, relating to Nathaniel's career after his "death" in 1967. It looked like the Russians had gotten closest to catching him, but he'd used the Chernobyl disaster to cover his tracks. Then the USSR had collapsed and they'd forgotten him. But one thing was for sure: Nathaniel was responsible for one nuclear disaster and now he was planning another.

She was still reeling from that knowledge. How could anyone be so ruthless? And how could anyone be so evil to do it again? She poured out another mug of bitter black coffee. It was cold now, but she hardly noticed. "Ian?"

Ian collected the key documents. "Amy will want to have a look at this."

Dmitry shook his head. "No flights now. Wait till morning."

Ian already had his cell out. "We can get a red-eye to Beijing if we hurry. Then we can swap on to a domestic flight that'll take us to Shanghai."

"No, little prince," said Dmitry. "You stay one more day. Much business to discuss."

"Dmitry, I'll pay you when I'm back in charge. I promise."

"Er . . . Ian," Cara went still as Dmitry turned to face them. "I think your last check must have bounced."

"What are you talking about?" Then Ian understood. Dmitry was pointing a gun at them.

Cara raised her hands and sat down.

Ian shook his head. "I'm disappointed, Dmitry. A double cross? I thought we were family."

How could Ian be so cool?

"Sit down, little prince. We wait." Dmitry craned his head to look past them, out of the window.

Ian glanced over his shoulder. "Reinforcements?"

Dmitry shrugged. "Not personal, little prince. Mice need cheeses."

"How much is Nathaniel paying you?" Ian asked. "I'll double it. I promise."

Dmitry smiled. It was warm and the sort of smile

an uncle might give a favorite nephew. "Ah, little prince. But I need money now. Not promises."

Cara heard cars pulling up outside. "Ian . . ."

Ian collected his briefcase. "We're leaving, Dmitry. You'll need to shoot us to stop us."

"No joking. You sit."

"No joke." Ian turned his steely gaze at Dmitry. "I don't find men pointing guns at me remotely funny. Out of my way, Dmitry."

Cara glared at Ian. "Sit down, Ian. Do as he says."

But Ian didn't listen. He was walking calmly forward, in the direction of Dmitry. He stepped right up to him, pressing his chest against the barrel of the pistol. "Out of my way or shoot."

That's it. He's finally gone insane.

Ian gazed up at Dmitry. "I'll count to three. Then I am going to hit you very hard."

"Ian!" Cara yelled.

"One . . ." counted Ian. He raised his briefcase. "Two . . ."

"Foolish little prince." Dmitry smiled, sadly.

And pulled the trigger.

CHAPTER 17

Nothing happened.

And Cara's heart started beating again.

Ian looked down at the pistol. "Disappointed, Dmitry. You are officially off my Christmas card list."

He swung the briefcase hard. It slammed into Dmitry's head with a sharp thud. Dmitry groaned but stayed upright. Ian hit him again. "Don't just stand there," he yelled at Cara. "Help me!"

Cara delivered a roundhouse kick and Dmitry was out.

Then she hugged Ian. "You stupid, stupid boy!" She drew apart and met his gaze. "You knew it was empty?"

Ian pulled a fistful of bullets from his pocket and tossed them away. "You know I don't like guns. Time to leave."

"Wait a minute." Cara grabbed the car keys. "Let's go."

They rushed along the corridor into the staircase. She heard footsteps down below, Dmitry's backup.

The elevator was still broken and this was the lone staircase. "The only way is up," she yelled.

Ian grabbed her hand and together they ran. They were panting by the time they reached the top floor and Cara kicked the roof door open.

"Nice view," said Ian. They were up high and Kiev at night sparkled brightly with lights.

Doors slammed open and men shouted from a few floors below. They were searching the apartment. He heard Dmitry yelling, then a heavy thump and Dmitry went silent.

"They don't sound happy," warned Ian.

Cara walked to the edge. "We need to get off this roof." She met Ian's eyes. "We have to jump. It's less than ten feet. Anyone could do it."

"I am not jumping! That's suicide."

"Says the boy who just marched up to a man with a pistol pointed at his heart."

"I'd taken out the bullets."

"And it never occurred to you he might reload?"

Ian gulped. He took a few steps back. "We jump?"

"On the count of three?"

Ian ran. He launched himself off the roof with a high-pitched scream, briefcase still in his hands. He galloped in midair, trying to gain more momentum, then down he came, crashing onto the opposite roof. Cara winced as he skidded in the gravel.

"That boy . . ."

And she jumped after him.

CHAPTER 18

Shanghai, China

"Jonah Wizard does not do incognito," said Jonah. "The world rocks to my beat; I am what I am!"

"And right now you're Phil Smith, research student at MIT," said Amy. She held up the bottle. "And this is going to happen."

Jonah stared at the bottle as if it were full of toxic waste, which it was, sort of.

Toxic waste for superstars.

Amy grinned. This wasn't *meant* to be fun, but she was having a great time.

Jonah backed away farther into the bathroom. "You're not qualified to do hair. Let me call my man in Beverly Hills. I'll fly him out here. He's the only one I trust to come near the Wizard scalp with a pair of clippers. I can't risk another repeat of . . . Sassoon-gate." He shuddered. "I thought I'd died."

"Sassoon-gate?" Amy asked. "Is that a thing?"

Jonah blanched. "It was the premiere of *Electro-Judge*, my homage to the classic disco era. My hairdresser had come down with some tropical disease while on-set at Angelina's latest, and they just let this *total* stranger cut my hair. An hour before I was to cruise the red carpet."

Ham shuddered. "You should have seen the tweets, Amy."

Jonah raised his hands to his head protectively. "It took me a month at my pad in the Seychelles to get over it."

Amy sighed. Famous people just didn't have the same problems as everyone else. "Jonah, we can't have Jonah Wizard parading around Shanghai. We've got the drop on Nathaniel, so this has to be done. I need to give you . . . a makeover."

"Just not my hair!" Jonah complained. "My image consultant took six months to design it!"

Amy pointed at the suit on the hotel bed. "And that is Phil Smith's look."

Jonah slumped over the sink. "Okay. Fine. I can do Method. So, where's the suit from? Dior? I'll settle for Tom Ford if it's silk."

Ham inspected the label. "Polyester and Lycra, bro."

Jonah gave a pitiful wail.

"Man up," said Amy. She flipped the bottle cap open.

Jonah stared at his reflection. "It's . . . horrible."

Amy nodded. "Sorry, it's the best I could do."

"No one would believe it's me."

"Which is kind of the point, isn't it?" She held out the glasses. "Now these."

"Do I have to?"

They were the cheapest, ugliest plastic frames she could find at the street market in downtown Shanghai. It hadn't been easy. Shanghai was top dollar, filled with designer shops and chic restaurants all along the Bund, its famous main street. Jonah's latest album was high on the Shanghai charts; his face seemed to be plastered on every wall and their entire plan would crumble to nothing if Nathaniel discovered he was out here.

Now bleached blond (badly) and wearing a suit that was too short in the arms and too long in the legs and way too wide around the waist, not even Jonah's most fanatical fan would recognize him.

Jonah put the glasses on.

Ham burst into laughter. And promptly fell off the bed. The room shook with his laughing. He slowly got it under control, saw Jonah again, then collapsed into a second round of hysterics.

"You look like a dork. Not a geek, which is sort of cool, but a total dork."

Amy handed out the invitations. "Here you go, Phil Smith. And here's one for you, Tod Jones," as she handed Ham his own specially forged invitation to the symposium. She checked hers. "And my name's Alice Munroe."

Jonah scowled. "You think these will work?"

"Cara based them on Dr. Peerless's own invitation. And she replaced his details with ours on the check-in system so, yes, these will work."

Ham grinned. "Hey, mine says I've got a PhD in sports mechanics! Cool!"

"Your mom would be so proud," Jonah replied sarcastically.

Amy reviewed the schedule. "The symposium lasts three days with a gala dinner at the end. There'll be lectures every day, starting with a meet-and-greet reception in an hour. Then straight into the first series of presentations. We need to keep an eye out for anything that may hint at nuclear power. If Nathaniel is planning something, it'll be connected with that."

Ham pointed at the list of events. "I want to go to the talk on bees. Maybe there'll be a free honey tasting?"

"Eyes on the prize," said Jonah. "We're here to stop a nuclear apocalypse, got it?"

Ham gave a mock salute. "Got it, Phil."

Shanghai gleamed. Amy sat by the window as the taxi took them through the new city. Gigantic towers of glass, chrome, and neon surrounded her from all sides, each launching light into the night sky so that it seemed carved with color.

Cranes scored the horizon like titanic herons. New towers were going up, and each higher than the last. Shanghai was in a hurry to catch up, and overtake, the other cities of the world. This was what the megacities of the future would look like.

And Nathaniel wanted to destroy it all.

Why? As an Ekat, doesn't he applaud all this?

Walls shimmered with paneling, huge devices that converted the sun's rays into electricity. Amy and the boys had even traveled from Pudong International Airport to central Shanghai on a magnetic levitation train, the only commercial one of its kind.

Amy had gotten word from Ian and Cara. The files they'd sent were grim reading and filled Amy with dread. Nathaniel had caused the Chernobyl disaster. If he'd done it once, she was convinced he'd be more than willing to do it again. But was it here, in Shanghai?

Tianlong Center unfurled before them. The entrance was guarded by two dragon carvings of green marble and the drive itself was a sinewy path through bamboo gardens and pools.

"Now, this is more like it," said Jonah. "The five-star treatment."

A marquee stood in the arrival courtyard, with lines of visitors awaiting registration before entering. How many could the center hold? Thousands, for sure.

Five minutes later they were tagged and through into the main building. A vast atrium rose ten floors toward a starry sky. One wall of glass faced the river, and Amy watched ferries, their lights aglow, drift silently along the oil-black water.

"Are you here for the science symposium?"

Amy turned to face a young Chinese woman. She smiled and offered her hand. "I'm Dr. Lin. Welcome to the Tianlong Center." She pointed toward the main corridor. "There are three talks about to begin. The first is on climate change and will be held in the Silver conference hall. Then we have the future of bees being presented in the Bronze hall—"

Amy ignored the wistful moan from Ham. "And the third?"

"I will be giving a presentation on the future of energy supply," said Dr. Lin. "That's in the Jade conference room, down three floors."

Amy nodded. "That's what we're here for."

CHAPTER 19

Amy and the guys put themselves near the back of the lecture hall, letting the real scientists and engineers crowd in the front row seats like boys at the Super Bowl.

Amy recognized a few from the files they had back at Cahill HQ. There were about fifty or so people in the Jade conference room, over half of them Ekats. A few looked over toward her, as if she rang some sort of bell, but with the big red-frame glasses and her hair covered with a baseball cap, Amy succeeded in staying anonymous.

Though not Ham. Dr. Lin had stood next to him in the elevator and then personally taken him to his seat and was, even while preparing the audio-visual equipment, glancing over at him, smiling.

Amy nudged him. "Hey, have you seen how—"

Ham chuckled. "Is she fluttering her eyelashes?"

Amy peered. "Yes. And flicking her hair. Want me to let her down gently?"

"No, let her dream." He sighed. "Sometimes being this handsome and ripped is a burden, y'know?"

"You're blushing!" said Amy. "Why are you staring at her?"

"Not her. Check out the guy on her left."

The lights dimmed.

"Looks like we're starting," said Amy.

Dr. Lin brushed her hand over the patch of wall and instantly a 3-D projection appeared, floating over the audience.

"Whoa," exclaimed Ham.

There was a smattering of applause.

Dr. Lin waved at the projection. The network grew, a vast web stretching out under a holographic Shanghai. The web grew wider, taking in the surrounding area, passing over hills and across valleys, linking town after town.

"The Chinese government is keenly aware of the problems of energy supply, for the world's energy problems are our problems also. Which brings us to the most fundamental problem we all face. Where will this future energy come from?"

The scientists sat up.

Amy leaned forward as the holograms transformed into a range of modern systems. First up were rows of oil fields, spewing black smoke into the sky. Then big coal stations and finally nuclear reactors. "Even the youngest child realizes the danger of reliance on fossil-fuel technologies. But we are not yet in that utopia of reliable, global green technology." She snapped her fingers. "And does the answer truly lie here?"

Wind farms drifted overhead, their massive propellers rotating lazily. Buildings covered with solar panels rose around the audience, then floating tidal generators. A scientist laughed as a school of holographic fish swam past, and through, him.

Dr. Lin walked among the images. "These systems are inefficient. A wind farm in Alaska will do Texas no good at all. Covering the Sahara with solar panels will not make a lightbulb in Sweden glow. Transmission loss through cabling is a physical fact. What is needed is clean, local power on a global basis. We are taking the first steps toward that goal by melding the potential of future technology with the best of current science."

Amy looked around the audience. There were murmurs among some of the scientists.

Dr. Lin smiled. "What I mean is hybrids. Building a better future from the foundations of the present."

"Come on, then, tell us!" shouted a woman from the back.

People laughed, and Dr. Lin bestowed a generous smile on the group. She shook her head. "Alas, I can tell you nothing. . . ."

The audience groaned. A few muttered "fraud" and "gimmickry."

Dr. Lin's smile broadened. "But I can certainly show you something."

The lights dimmed. The far wall began to open. It split in the middle and drew away. A warm breeze blew across the room and lights shone from the other side of the wall. Bright, industrial-scale lights.

"Stay close," Amy suggested.

Ham nodded. He kept casual, but Amy picked up the subtle signs that he'd switched into "bodyguard" mode: his eyes scanning for threats, limbs loose and ready to react to any hint of trouble. Ham was different. When everyone else got tense at the hint of danger, he grew more relaxed. As if this was his natural state of being. His muscles were honed for a reason. To respond to and deal with danger, whatever its form. Ham had the ability of knowing trouble was here before it had even pressed the doorbell.

The wall opened up to reveal a large, busy control room. There was a glowing digital map on one wall; the others were lined with banks of control panels and screens. One wall was made up of glass, and beyond that was a vast underground chamber. A hundred yards below them was a series of huge semicircular enclosures.

"Steam turbines," muttered one of the engineers in the audience. He stood up to have a better look. "We're in some power station."

Dr. Lin summoned them forward. "Not any power station, but one unique to China, to the world. The world's first hybrid fission-fusion nuclear reactor."

"Uh-oh," said Jonah.

CHAPTER 20

The Black Forest, Germany

"Dan's gone? How?" Nellie stared at Sammy. "Did you check everywhere?"

"Everywhere," Sammy insisted. "He's not on the train."

They'd known something was wrong when they'd discovered they'd been locked into their compartment. It had taken some banging on the door and the conductor with the emergency key to get them out. Then the saga of the dining car. One of the passengers had heard gunshots, and a bullet hole was discovered in the wall. Nellie had managed to slip in and found, alongside the bullet hole, their map and guidebook.

"He was in the dining car when it all kicked off," she said, trying to piece the clues together. "And the passenger said she heard the shot around four A.M."

Sammy checked his watch. "Three hours ago."

"The conductor wants us all to stay aboard for the police in Stuttgart."

Sammy shook his head. "That'll slow us down, and what can we tell them? We need to find Dan."

"How? Assuming he got off at four in the morning, he's had three hours to move, or be moved."

Sammy glanced out the window. "Stuttgart's dead ahead. If we're going to do something, we need to do it now."

Had Dan gone off on his own? Nellie dismissed that immediately. He'd never leave without telling them. And someone had put a bullet in that wall.

No, he'd been taken, or someone had tried to take him. Nellie racked her brain. Where could Dan be? If he'd run, where would he run to? If he'd been taken, where would they take him?

They had to find him. Every atom of her body hummed to that purpose, that desire. Dan was alone, he needed them.

But how? She looked down each path and each one was a dead end. Nellie's heart was being torn in two.

The train was slowing down. The platform ahead was empty but for a handful of policemen. She had to decide what to do before they reached the station.

"Pack up. Fast," ordered Nellie.

"You've got a plan?"

"Yeah. The same as before. We find out what's at this location in Grace's blackmail file."

"We're not going after Dan?" Sammy sounded stunned.

"Believe me, I don't want to do this." Nellie folded up the map and tucked it into her combat pants. She felt sick; it was as if she was betraying Dan. "If I had a clue, a *single* clue, to which way Dan had gone, then I'd follow it." Her guidebook went into the top of her backpack. "But I don't. So we do what we were sent here to do. Dan will have to find us."

"How?"

"He was looking at the map, Sammy. The boy's got a photographic memory. We don't know where he is, but he knows where we'll be."

The train stopped. As the police boarded from the left, Nellie activated the emergency door release on the right and disembarked onto the opposite platform. With their backpacks and trekking gear they looked like any of the hundred or so students and hikers already milling around in the station.

They found the car rental just outside, and twenty minutes later they loaded their backpacks into the trunk and were heading south on the A81, Nellie at the wheel, Sammy riding shotgun.

Nellie peered into the rearview mirror. "You see that gunmetal gray BMW? Two cars back?"

"Yeah."

"I think it's been following us since the train station."

"You sure?"

"No," she replied. "Just a thin line between being paranoid and—"

"Getting kidnapped off a moving train in the middle of the night?"

Nellie glanced over. "Something like that."

Sammy pointed at a sign. "Pull into that gas station." He looked back as they slowed down. "Definitely following."

He was right. The BMW was signaling to pull in, too.

"Park by the shop," said Sammy. "I'm going to grab some snacks. Want anything?"

"Are you serious?" But Nellie did what Sammy said.

She watched the BMW from the mirror. It was waiting at the other end of the parking area.

Sammy was taking his time.

There were two guys in the car. Neither looked interested in getting out.

Nellie jumped as the door burst open. Sammy slid in and handed over a half-empty bag of marshmallows. "Want one?"

"What is going on?"

"Just drive." He had a grin on his face that meant trouble for someone.

Nellie twisted the keys and began to reverse out. "You ate those real quick."

Sammy held up the bag. "No. I've had two. Most of them are shoved up the exhaust pipe of that beautiful car."

"What?"

"Oh, and an orange, too. Just to be sure."

Nellie laughed as they rejoined the autobahn. She could just glimpse the BMW, still stationary in the parking area. "Why the marshmallows?"

"To stop the orange from rolling out. The exhaust was hot, the marshmallows would melt in seconds, and you know how sticky a molten marshmallow is. You don't need to be a genius to think it through."

Nellie glanced over to him. "But it helps, right?"

Sammy grinned. "It does indeed."

CHAPTER 21

Sammy hoisted his backpack out of the trunk of their rental car. "Looks like we're walking from here."

Nellie looked into the forest and decided she was totally a city girl. It looked grim and foreboding. Her red hoodie seemed like an omen. "But Granny told me to never, ever stray off the path."

Sammy grinned. "What does your granny know about forests? She grew up in Brooklyn."

Nellie buckled on her own pack and joined Sammy at the edge of the road. "How far is it?"

Sammy inspected the map, then pointed. "Eleven miles, northwest. We'll be camping out tonight."

"Then we'd better get a move on," she said.

The canopy blocked out the sun but trapped in the heat. The breeze didn't make it down to ground level, making the air thick and heavy. Insects busied themselves, and the forest was filled with their monotonous droning.

Nellie's new boots chafed and she felt the sweat trickle down her back. She reached for her water bottle and found it already half empty. How far had they gone? Not even a mile.

It felt old, this place. Old and full of memories. The trees crowded around them, their branches creaking in the breeze, as if they were old men whispering among themselves. The boughs loomed low, with spindly, long fingers, dark and twisted. The moss-covered rocks had sunk in deep—they had settled there since the last ice age and weren't in the mood to go anywhere soon. The trees that had died left their rotten trunks and were a breeding ground for yellow and green toadstools. The musky smell made Nellie think of predators.

She chattered at first, keeping them both distracted from the hard slog. And hard it was. The earth was soft and each step needed to be dragged out. There were fallen trunks to be clambered over and streams to be jumped. The ground rolled up and down, forcing them to scurry up slopes on their hands and knees and creep down slopes, watching for roots and holes that could easily snap an ankle if they weren't careful.

After a couple of hours her talk ceased. Nellie walked, head down, breathing heavily as they plowed on. The pair stopped every few minutes to check their GPS and the map, try to smile at each other, then march on.

Nellie's clothes were drenched. She wanted a cool dip in some lovely, fairy-tale pool. But the only water they found was brown and algae-covered and stinking.

Sammy stopped by a mound of ivy covering

what appeared to be a boulder. "Look at what I've found."

"Let me guess. A gingerbread house?"

He pulled at a handful of vine. "It's a Jeep."

Nellie helped drag off the upper layer of foliage. After a few minutes they'd revealed the hood and a twisted, broken windshield.

The rust had eaten away much of the metal but what was left remained an army green. Sammy got out a utility knife and scraped away at the license plate. "Registration's from 1965. Military."

"Think it's got something to do with the research facility?" Nellie asked. But there was nothing else around here except for trees and more trees. Certainly no buildings or any signs of an encampment or base. She sighed. Maybe there was nothing left here to find; it had been over fifty years.

Sammy tapped his map. "Grace kept these coordinates for something." He stood up. "Come on. Let's get as far as we can before nightfall."

They managed to cover another five miles before the shadows took control of the forest. The lack of light turned the uneven ground into an obstacle course. They stumbled over hidden roots every dozen yards, and tripped over a buried rock every twenty.

Sammy took off his backpack. "That's it, Nellie, we're not going any farther."

"But we've only got another four miles left."

He stretched. "And we're averaging two miles an hour. We stop here and hit our goal tomorrow morning. I've read too many fairy tales to go wandering around forests at night. This place gives me the creeps."

Nellie took off her own backpack and flipped open the top. "There's only one way of dealing with the creeps." She dug deep into her pack and found her stash. She pulled it out and handed it over. "Here we go."

"Candy?" said Sammy. "I was expecting something with a trigger."

"Not mere candy, Belgian chocolate. Made in Bruges."

Sammy snapped the bar and peeled off the wrapper. "I don't see—"

"Wait a minute. You do not just stuff handmade chocolate with eighty-five-percent cocoa content in your mouth like that." She shook a packet of ground coffee. "Get a fire started."

"This. Is. Amazing," said Sammy.

The sun was long gone. The tent was up, a green camo number that they'd grabbed on the way up here. The fire was bright and warm and working on getting their dinner ready.

"For a science geek, you're pretty outdoorsy," said Nellie.

"Plenty of trips out into the desert to view the stars," Sammy replied. "You bring the chocolate, I'll bring the telescope."

Nellie watched the dancing flames. Her head

dipped. A yawn stretched out of her mouth. She knew she should move to the tent but her limbs were just too heavy to be bothered to carry her the three yards to where her sleeping bag lay. She let the flames warm her toes, wiggling free after a day packed in her hiking boots.

Sammy sat up. "Hear that?"

Blinking, Nellie shook the sleep fuzz out. "What?"

Sammy didn't speak. He stood up slowly, quietly, back to the flames so he could search the darkness.

A crack of a twig. The groan of a branch bending and leaves shaking as something brushed past.

Nellie gripped a frying pan.

The air quivered with a soft, predatory growl.

A wolf?

Nellie swallowed. Meeting a wolf in the woods was not on her bucket list.

The line of trees broke up the cast of the firelight. The unsteady flames made the ground seem to move, the shadows jump.

But there was definitely something out there. . . .

And it was big. Really big.

A bear?

Pale yellow eyes stared out from under a shadowy brow and Nellie shivered as the creature snarled, its cracked lips parting to reveal crooked, ivory fangs.

"I wish you'd packed a bazooka," whispered Sammy, trying to hide his fear in a bad joke.

It prowled at the edge of their campfire; Nellie dared not move. The best she could do was slant sideways and see the sweat trickle down Sammy's forehead.

The creature snorted, and then the twigs crunched and trees shook as it lumbered away.

And Nellie breathed again. "What was it?"

Sammy stared at his shaking hands and turned them into fists to try to still them. He met her gaze. "Nothing good."

CHAPTER 22

Somehow Nellie slept. She woke with the birds, and the glow of morning sunlight filled the tent.

Sammy's sleeping bag was empty.

She jerked up and ran out. "Sammy? Sammy?"

"Here."

Nellie went to where he was crouched and slapped his head. "Do not go off like that. I thought—"

"Look at this." He pointed to a mark on the ground.

The leaves had been pushed into the mossy earth. The shape had sprung back an inch or two,

but it was some sort of paw print. Sammy spread his hand over it. "Not even close. The thing was huge. A monster."

"They have bears in this part of the world."

"Have a look."

Sammy was right; they were big paw prints, and the beast had claws longer than her finger. But there was something odd about them. . . .

She frowned. There had to be an explanation. "Maybe it doubled back a few paces."

Sammy shook his head. "No. See how the front paws are sunk deeper in? That's because it was moving forward. So that raises an important question, doesn't it?"

Nellie recounted the prints in the mud. "What sort of animal has six legs?"

Despite the creeping heat, Nellie shivered. "I don't want to hang around here any longer. Let's get this over and done with."

Sammy stood up. He didn't look well rested. "Whatever's out here better be worth it."

It didn't take long to pack and be on their way. Their gear was lighter; there was less food and water, and Nellie hoped that they'd make it back before things got desperate. But if she'd hoped they'd make quicker time, she was sadly mistaken. The ground became rougher and denser as they ventured deeper into the heart of the forest.

It was midafternoon when they came across it.

The fence.

Vines had crawled over the links and the bare metal was rusted through and through. The upper section had been wound with barbed wire, but that was now just covered in windblown moss, great clumps hanging down from the spikes like some green headdress.

A rusty sign dangled from its one remaining nail.

"'*Verboten*,'" read Nellie. "Forbidden."

"Yeah, kinda guessed that." Sammy pointed up high. "Check out the watchtowers."

They slipped through one of the tears in the perimeter fence and came across what had first appeared as small hillocks but were actually outbuildings, now covered in foliage. They had rotted through, their roofs collapsed and broken up by the relentless mark of time and tree roots. The whole site had a damp, forgotten odor. Nellie spotted another abandoned Jeep and, hidden within the trees, a few more outbuildings. The forest had claimed this place back, and it hadn't taken long.

Sammy spotted a rusty tank. He hammered it, listening to the dull echo, then pointed up to a vine-covered flue. "Generator. Still has some fuel."

Twenty or so yards beyond was a hillside with a steel door set into it. The wind had blown decades' worth of leaves and other detritus up against it, and it was pitted with age and corrosion.

And it was open.

"I'm not sure that's good or bad," said Sammy.

"The pneumatics look like they corroded," he said, inspecting the doors. "No pressure to keep them shut so they just rolled open."

They approached the main building. It was windowless, built of solid concrete, and seemed to extend into the side of a low hill.

Nellie kicked the wall. "Looks like a bomb shelter." She wrinkled her nose as she peered into the darkness beyond. "You smell that?" It was more than just stale air. It was foul, like a chemistry experiment gone wrong.

"It would be hard not to." He unclipped his flashlight from his belt. "Well, this is the address. Let's go check it out."

Cobwebs surrounded the lighting fixtures. The walls and floor were bare concrete, painted a faded khaki. Long tin ducts ran along the ceiling and there was a vast web of wiring, crisscrossing above them, strung out from old trunking down corridors that branched off from this central spine. Alongside the ducts were lines of pipes, big, small, color-coded. Doors, steel-plated, ran along both sides, neatly and identically spaced with regimental precision.

Sammy gazed around in awe. "Wow. A bona fide Cold War secret base. I've read about them but never thought I'd ever get a chance to explore one." He clicked with his cell. "Now, this is going on my Facebook page."

"Be serious, Sammy."

"Hey, if it isn't on Facebook it never happened."

Nellie brushed aside a cobweb from a sign-board. "It's in German and English."

"We're on the side that would have been West Germany, so that's not odd. If we'd been across the border, the signs would have been in German and Russian," Sammy noted.

"But why is it here? And what was Nathaniel up to?"

"See these pipes?" Sammy stuck his thumb up.

"Yes. What about them?"

He reached up and tapped one. "This is nitrogen oxide. This is oxygen. Then we've got carbon dioxide in here and methane in this one. All empty by now, but this is identical to what we've got running along the corridors in our university science department."

"You're saying we're in some laboratory?"

Sammy nodded. "And this is where I tell you I've got a bad feeling about this. Look." He shone his flashlight along the wall. "A place like this would have emergency backup."

The light swept onto a large steel control panel. Sammy wiped off the dust and cobwebs and inspected the buttons. "And let there be light." He flipped a row of switches.

The wiring over their heads crackled, and sparks jumped from the sockets. From outside Nellie heard the old generator splutter to life, its pistons pushing against decades' worth of grime. But fitfully some of the lights came on.

There was still plenty of darkness, like in the corridor to their left. Sammy checked it with his flashlight.

The corridor ended with a steel doorway. Beside it was a row of moth-eaten hazmat suits and a shower, used in case of contamination. Beneath the suits were rubber boots, all rotted through and home for mice.

"Uh-oh," muttered Sammy, staring at the sign on the steel door facing them.

The door was marked with the yellow-and-black trefoil, the international symbol for radiation.

"You think we should go in?" said Nellie.

"I'd rather not."

Nellie picked one of the suits off its hook. There was a name tag sewn onto its breast. "I really think we should."

She showed Sammy the tag.

It read MAJOR NATHANIEL HARTFORD.

CHAPTER 23

Shanghai, China

The audience made their way into the control room. They were stunned into silence.

"Please, no photos," said Dr. Lin. "The owners would like to keep their technology a secret for now."

"Owners?" asked Amy.

"A partnership between the Chinese government and private industrialists."

Amy gazed up. "And this reactor is right under Shanghai?"

"One hundred and four meters," answered Dr. Lin. "As I previously said, transmission losses through cabling can reduce supply by around thirty percent on average. So by building stations closer to point of use, we save considerable energy, allowing us to build smaller, more cost-effective stations. What you see here is as much a research facility as it is a power station. We intend to solve the riddle of fusion once and for all."

"Nuclear fusion?" asked Ham.

Dr. Lin smiled at him. "All nuclear power stations at present operate on the principle of energy released through fission, splitting atoms. But fusion, the reaction that powers the sun itself, releases energy by joining atoms. And the energy produced by fusion is three times greater than by fission."

"And it's clean," added one of the other scientists as he inspected the control panels. "You've managed to do that?"

Dr. Lin frowned. "The system is in place, and we have had moderate success. It provides a small percentage of the city's energy, almost five percent."

"And the rest of the time you run on good old fission?" said Jonah.

Dr. Lin met his gaze. "By the end of the year we are on target to double the fusion output." She clapped her hands. "Now for the tour. Would you follow the guides to the elevators outside? I have the head of engineering waiting below to show you the turbines."

There were only three elevators and everyone was trying to be first. Dr. Lin smiled apologetically at Amy. "They are like schoolboys, yes?"

Amy grinned. If Sammy was here he'd have been deep in the scrum, too.

Dr. Lin shrugged and pointed to an elevator off to the side of the corridor. "Let's take the freight elevator. It's just as quick, and a short walk will have us in the engineering department ahead of the rest."

She took her ID tag and swiped the keypad. The doors opened and they stepped into a plain box lined with dented sheet steel.

The door closed.

Dr. Lin pressed the lowest level. Amy noticed her hand tremble. "We're going farther down?" asked Amy.

Dr. Lin smiled stiffly. "Yes."

She's sweating. Something's wrong.

Dr. Lin backed into a corner.

"Ham . . ." Amy warned.

"On it." Ham pushed her and Jonah behind him.

The elevator stopped.

The door opened.

It happened so suddenly, so quickly, Amy didn't even have time to scream.

Alek Spasky was waiting. He held his pistol close to his body but pointed at them.

Ham charged.

The muzzle flashed and the explosion of gunpowder was deafening within the small steel confines of the elevator. Blood spurted from Ham's left shoulder, but that didn't stop him.

Ham grabbed Alek and there was a second shot, muffled compared to the first. Ham grunted as the bullet tore into his thigh.

Dr. Lin screamed.

The air was filled with the stink of burned gunpowder.

Ham punched Alek so hard it took him off his feet. His gun clattered along the bare concrete floor of the corridor.

But Ham had two bullets in him. His next blow was wild, and Alek reacted with a double chop into Ham's throat. Ham gasped and hit the floor.

Jonah and Amy lunged at Alek. Jonah ran, head down, smacking Alek in the gut. Amy swung her leg into the back of Alek's knee, hoping to bring him down.

Alek pushed Jonah into the way of her attack and all she ended up doing was kicking him in the head. Jonah spun on the spot, unconscious.

Two down in as many seconds.

But there was no time to pause.

A backhand blow caught Amy on the forehead and she was knocked against the steel wall of the elevator. She clawed at it, trying to stay standing. Her head pulsed with pain.

Through blurry eyes she watched Alek pick up his pistol.

Do something, Cahill.

She took a wobbly step toward Alek, desperate to wrestle the pistol away. He merely glanced over his shoulder and kicked her legs out from under her.

She tried to get up but Alek pointed the pistol at her and shook his head. "On your knees."

Slowly, with her hands raised, Amy did as she was told. She glanced at the others. Ham was bleeding badly, Jonah was unconscious. "My friends, they need help."

"Hardly my concern. Time to die, Ms. Cahill."

CHAPTER 24

The hard muzzle of the pistol pressed against Amy's head.

Her breath came in panicked half gasps—she struggled as though she'd forgotten how to breathe.

"Don't move, Ms. Cahill," said Alek Spasky.

Move? She could barely think. She didn't trust her body to do anything.

"I've done this before," continued Alek. "A few times, actually. You are afraid, delirious with terror. That is normal. Calm yourself. Accept your fate. Make your last seconds . . . sublime."

"S-sublime?" He was talking nonsense.

"I have traveled the world, investigated every religion, every philosophy. They all teach the same thing. How to embrace this moment of your life. The last. Savor it, Ms. Cahill, the exquisiteness of life. The air tastes different, yes?"

Now that he said it, Amy realized he was right. Air had a taste. She'd never noticed it before. "How?"

"That's because now you take nothing for granted."

Amy forced her body under control. She had to do something. She tensed her arm. If she could spin around . . .

Alek huffed. "No. The trigger is very sensitive. It requires little pressure."

Amy had one last shot. She slowly shifted her head. Alek responded by pushing the muzzle deeper. Amy tried not to sob. She needed every ounce of self-control. "Is this what Natalia would have wanted?"

Was that a sudden intake of breath? Or was she so desperate she'd imagined it?

Ever so slowly, she tried to turn her head. To see the others.

Jonah was unconscious, but she could hear a soft groan as he struggled to wake. Dr. Lin was curled up, terrified, but had wrapped her scarf around Ham's leg wound and had her hands pressed on the bullet hole in his shoulder. Ham himself looked pale and barely conscious. He needed a hospital.

"How do you know about Natalia?"

"That you had a wife? Does it matter?"

"No, I suppose not. Now that she is dead."

"Dead but not forgotten. And still loved. Why else the roses?" said Amy. "She's been dead thirty years."

"You know nothing about Natalia, nor me."

"I know she was a hero. And that you loved her very much and maybe, just maybe, your life would have been very different if she'd not gone to Chernobyl."

"I warned her not to go. She didn't listen."

"She saved thousands and thousands of lives, Alek."

"And how did they reward her sacrifice?" She'd never heard Alek angry, but now that she had, Amy knew she had to tread very carefully. "A lead-lined coffin."

"She was what all Ekats strive to be, Alek. Willing to do anything to make the world a better place. Is there a better legacy than that? Any truer member of the Cahill family?"

"It's the Cahill legacy that destroyed her. That filled her mind with ridiculous ambitions."

"No. It's the Cahill legacy that made her the woman you loved," said Amy. "The ambition to do good is never ridiculous."

Alek didn't respond. Had she pushed him too far? Amy tensed. Would she feel it?

This wasn't sublime—kneeling, waiting for death. It was sad, pathetic, and humiliating.

"Is this how you honor her?" said Amy. "Planning a second meltdown?"

"What do you mean?"

"The bomb. You intend to blow up this power station."

The pistol barrel pushed farther against her head. "Is that what you believe? That I would go along with such . . . an atrocity?"

"But we know you're planning a bombing."

Alek laughed. "Oh, a small explosive device, yes. That will remove the top floor of the Hilton at the gala dinner. Just enough to wipe out the guests at the symposium."

"The Ekat branch."

"Yes. The Ekat branch."

Amy didn't know whether to laugh or cry.

They weren't planning to cause a second meltdown. This entire ruse was to get the Ekats in one place and kill them with a simple bomb. She should feel relieved, the city was safe. But still, hundreds would die. She would die.

And yet, why here? Why hold a symposium here, in Shanghai, with an actual nuclear reactor right under everyone's feet? "Nathaniel asked you to do this?"

"Of course."

Why? Why bring everyone here? Why get Alek to plant a bomb, a mere bomb?

Unless . . .

"It's a double cross, Alek," said Amy. "He's going to sabotage the reactor. That was always his plan. And he'll use it to get rid of you."

There was a pause. "Even Nathaniel wouldn't do something so monstrous." But Amy could hear the doubt in his voice. "Get up."

Amy blinked. What had he just said?

"Get up, Amy Cahill," said Alek. "Get up and turn around."

She did, slowly and with her hands still raised.

He'd stepped back, just out of arm's reach, and the pistol was still aimed squarely at her. Alek's eyes were narrowed with suspicion, as if he was wondering if this was some ploy of Amy's to extend her life by a brief minute or two.

"You should be proud of her, Alek. What she did in her short life is greater than what most will do if they lived to be a hundred. She's achieved more than you, that's for certain."

Alek's eyes hardened. "It's foolish to taunt a man aiming a gun at your heart."

"If you're going to kill me, then I'd rather it was because I told you the truth."

"And what truth is that?"

"That Chernobyl was no accident. It was sabotage." Amy raised her head and lowered her arms. Whatever happened next, she wasn't going to face it cowering. "And carried out on the orders of Nathaniel Hartford."

Alek's eyes widened it shock. He stared, stunned all the way through, but then shook his head, shaking off the weakness Amy had just glimpsed. "A lie. A desperate and feeble lie. I expected better."

"What do you think Nathaniel's been doing all these years? Do you honestly think he was just waiting for Grace to die? Of course not! He's been prodding her defenses! You look back, unblinkered, and you'll see all the trial runs, all the disasters and mishaps he threw at her, just to see if he could break her. But he couldn't, not Grace. That doesn't change the fact that he arranged Chernobyl."

Amy wasn't sure if she'd convinced Alek. He would guess she'd try anything to live, and maybe even use his wife's memory against him. She pointed at her pocket. "It's all on my cell. Ian sent me the old KGB documents regarding the 'accident.' Nathaniel's fingerprints are all over it."

"Take out your cell. Slowly."

She did. Alek snatched it from her. He took a step back, out of range in case she tried to lunge for him. He scanned the documents, his eyes narrowing with cold rage as he read about the stolen radioactive materials, the hunt for the arms smugglers. Amy saw his jaw tighten.

"The photo is of Nathaniel. There is no mistake." His shoulders sank. "What a fool I've been."

Amy shifted her gaze to the pistol still pointed at her. What would Alek do now? She was afraid, now that he knew the truth. He'd take it out on her. This was the chance, the one small chance, to make Alek see what had been going on. To make him change his mind about what he planned to do. Amy needed to say something, something clever and powerful that would make the difference at this very moment. But then she realized this was no time to be clever. This was the time to be honest.

"Help me, Alek."

He lowered his pistol. He looked weary. "Go, little Cahill. Go and die another day."

Amy's mind was racing almost as fast as her heartbeat. "But he'll only send others, once he knows you've failed. And he won't trust you, either, will he?"

"What do you mean?"

"We need to make him stop chasing me," said Amy, a plan coming together. An awful one.

"Can you contact Nathaniel?"

"He was expecting me to call him when this business was completed." Alek drew out his own cell. "You want to speak to him?"

Amy met Alek's gaze. "I want him to see me die."

Alek didn't reply, not immediately. He observed her, and Amy guessed he was calculating the likelihood of her scheme actually working.

Then he smiled, his blue eyes cold as ice. "This had better work, for your sake."

Amy ruffled up her hair. She had to make this look good. She switched off a few of the lights; the gloom would help disguise any . . . theatrical failings. It's not like she faked her death regularly.

Alek looked at her. "Good. But you're missing something."

"What?"

His backhand blow swept her off her feet. Amy lay there, head ringing with pain, her body trembling with shock.

"A sense of fear," said Alek. "You are now pumping adrenaline, your eyes are dilated with the primal survival urge, fight or flight." He turned to the screen as it flickered to life. "Nathaniel? I have someone for you. I've captured Amy Cahill."

Amy got to her feet but the ground seemed to bend. She blinked, trying to clear the tears. Her cheekbone burned and she felt the birth of a bruise just under her eye. Alek didn't fool around.

"Yes, she's right here." Alek shoved the cell at her. "There is someone wanting to speak with you."

Amy took the cell.

The screen flickered and buzzed. She wiped the tears from her eyes. The image came into view. She gasped.

"Dan?"

This wasn't the plan! He looked unharmed, and Amy almost cheered. He stared, confused, into the screen. The reception down here was breaking up the image. "Dan!"

He frowned, struggling with the sound. Then his eyes widened. A look of pure horror spread across his face. Amy wanted to tell him everything was fine, that this was just a trick, that she was on her way, but she couldn't breathe a word, not with Nathaniel mere feet away from Dan.

She glanced up at Alek. He put his hand over the screen.

"If you make *him* believe, then Nathaniel will believe."

"But he's my brother. I can't have him think I'm dead! It will destroy him!" She could hear him shouting her name. He sounded so afraid.

"You have so little faith in Dan? You must go through with it. If Nathaniel suspects, even for a moment, that this is some ruse, then he will lock himself up so tightly, rearrange his plans, and we'll never stop him. This is our only chance to finish Nathaniel Hartford *once and for all*. It will give us the chance we need to reach Nathaniel with his defenses down."

"But I can't lie to Dan—"

"You *have* to." He slowly lifted his hand away.

He was right. It was tearing her heart in two to see the pain and hopelessness on Dan's face, but she didn't have any choice. She had to convince him she was about to die. She shook the cell. "Dan! Dan! Can you hear me?"

He stared back at her, ashen-faced. "Amy! I'm here!"

"I—I don't have much time, Dan. You have to listen . . ."

Alek switched off the cell and helped Amy off the floor. "He was convinced. Well done."

Amy's veins pulsed with horror. "My brother thinks I'm dead."

"Yes, he does. I hope that does not make him do anything foolish."

She hadn't thought of that. What would she do if she'd just seen Dan, apparently, die? Amy bit her lip. "Do you know where he is?"

The lights faltered. For a second they went out, plunging the corridor into utter darkness. Then the emergency lights flickered, spilling their red, hellish glow over the five of them.

Then the alarms sounded.

Dr. Lin stared at the lights, her face pale. "No, no, no!"

Alek gripped the doctor's arm. "What's going on?"

"It's a level-four alarm!" she screamed. "We need to run!"

Jonah blinked into consciousness. He gazed about him, then saw Ham. "Bro!" He knelt beside him. "He's bleeding! We've got to do something!"

Ham smiled weakly. "I'm all right. Just need to get up. Get moving." He glanced at his bloody leg. "It's only a little hole."

Dr. Lin was struggling in Alek's grasp, trying to flee.

"How far could you run?" said Amy. "A mile? Two? Not far enough to escape."

Alek looked at her coldly. "I underestimated you, Amy Cahill. And I trusted Nathaniel. Two mistakes I won't make again. Though I fear we are too late."

Amy was up on her feet. "There has to be a chance."

Dr. Lin shook her head. "We need to run!"

"We need to stop this!" Amy shouted. "You have to help us!"

Dr. Lin blinked. "How?"

Alek Spasky gestured at the elevator. "The control room. Take us there. Once we know what the problem is, perhaps we can fix it." He waved his pistol at the elevator door. "Quickly, Dr. Lin."

Jonah looked up. "What about Ham?"

Dr. Lin pointed at an elevator along the corridor. "There is a medical facility on the top floor. If they've gone already, you'll find bandages."

Jonah nodded and, together with Amy, lifted the big Tomas to his feet.

Thousands of thoughts rushed through her mind, and thousands of emotions—raw, overwhelming, and terrifying—flooded her heart. There was so much she wanted to say. "Jonah, I don't know how this is going to turn out . . ." she started, trying not to choke on what the words meant. "I don't know how to say good-bye. . . ."

Jonah gripped her hand. He squeezed it so tightly she thought she felt her bones crack. "So don't."

Amy stepped into the service elevator, joining Alek and Dr. Lin.

To try to stop a nuclear meltdown.

CHAPTER 25

The Black Forest, Germany

Nathaniel's secret was here, Nellie knew it. The secret Grace had discovered that forced her to order his death.

Through the steel door the first things they found were the cages. They ranged from boxes about a foot cubed, to containers large enough for something the size of a bull. Each one had a clipboard hanging from it: some bare, others with yellowed paper and circled-up black-and-white photographs.

Nellie picked one up. It was a laboratory report on a beagle. Stamped across each page in red was a single word.

The next was a report on a three-year-old chimpanzee.

An Alsatian puppy.

Some of the cages were large, human-size. Nellie approached one of them and saw the report was on a family of bears. Of the three, two had "failed." Nellie couldn't stand to look anymore. "Animal testing. But what was being tested?"

Sammy had one of the clipboards and was giving it a critical analysis. "We're looking at a dark time in warfare, Nellie. The arms race was on in a big way. Remember, this is the era of the Cuban missile crisis and nukes lining up along the border between East and West; we're right at the battlefront. It wasn't just nukes they were worried about, but chemical and biological warfare. This looks like a test labora-tory for . . . all sorts of unpleasant stuff."

"Nathaniel's doing?"

Sammy waved the clipboard. "His signature's on every one of these. Looks like he was boss."

"Boss of what?"

Sammy looked around. "We forget, but back in the day, people thought nuclear energy was the answer to everything. Cheap electricity, threaten-ing your enemies, ending wars. And medicine. Radiation's used to treat a number of diseases. All that knowledge came out of this era. Maybe Nathaniel went . . . further."

"How?"

"Radiation treatment can cure, it can kill. It alters the DNA of the subject. It causes—"

"Mutations," said Nellie. She'd read enough comics to know the basics. "You think that was what Nathaniel was trying to do here? Create mutants?"

Sammy's eyes widened. "Give me that report again. The one on the chimp." Sammy searched through the pages. "Listen to this. 'The subject began to display signs of enhanced mental aptitude, com-pleting the puzzles thirty-five percent more quickly than prior to the treatment. Its physical strength had risen by thirty-seven percent, and its agility and hand-eye coordination improved by twenty-nine percent. Tomorrow we shall increase the period in the radiation dose by another forty percent to see if these attributes can be further enhanced.'" He flipped over the page. "Ah. They increased the dose, but the animal couldn't take it. The experiment 'failed.'"

Nellie gazed at the empty cages. "Brain power. Strength. Agility. You know what that reminds me of?"

"It's like the thirty-nine clues serum! It does exactly the same thing—enhances a person's abilities to superhuman." Sammy folded the sheets away in his pocket. "So that was Nathaniel's plan all along. He couldn't access the original formula, so he thought he could replicate the results with radiation technology."

"A modern-day Victor Frankenstein."

"That's what Grace meant," concluded Sammy. "Who would have supported Nathaniel, knowing this was what he was up to? Who would want to go through this just to have the abilities the serum would give you?"

"And this was what Hope stumbled onto. Poor girl." Nellie could only imagine the nightmares such a place would give a six-year-old. Wandering around here, the sick animals in their cages. "Come on, we've got the proof we need. This place gives me the creeps."

"There might be more." Sammy was looking down the darkened corridor beyond.

"Don't you think we've seen enough?"

Sammy set his lips in a grim line. "We can't risk missing anything, Nellie."

Nellie swallowed, and on they went.

The next room was protected by an air lock, useless now, but once it would have been up and running to make sure whatever was inside didn't get out. Nellie slid the plate-glass door aside and shone the flashlight in.

Surgical tools had been left in their trays. There was a huge operating light overhead; its ten lenses made Nellie think of a giant insect peering down at them. It hung over an operating table.

The floor was tiled, for ease of cleaning, yet Nellie felt her stomach churn at the dark brown patches and the clogged floor drain.

There were bones in the corners, and bedding. Mattresses and sheets had been dragged into a pile. Sammy inspected one of the larger bones. "This is deer. It's been gnawed at."

Nellie sniffed the air, smelling something on top of the stale dust. A moist, animal musk. "This is a den."

"I've got a bad feeling about this. . . ." He locked his hand into hers. "Let's go."

Sammy was right. They knew what they needed to know.

They got moving fast, back into the corridor and toward the exit. Nellie needed to be out of this place. Now where was the door? She turned and—

Nellie saw it, just a blur as her flashlight caught a sudden motion, the shining ivory color of claws and fangs. She screamed as it ripped into Sammy.

CHAPTER 26

Sammy lay motionless, blood seeping through the clothing on his back.

Nellie stepped back, her gaze trapped by the creature's.

It was the thing that prowled the camp last night.

It moved on all six limbs. The two pairs of arms were long but spindly, but its legs were thick—muscle-bound and coiled for leaping. The skin was raw, red, and covered with lumps.

What was it? It was like nothing she'd ever seen.

It growled and edged forward; its small yellow eyes blazed with bloodlust.

Was Sammy alive? The creature's claws were five inches long and sharp as scalpels.

It rose up onto its rear legs and Nellie stifled a scream.

It was a bear, but not one found in nature. As well as its normal set of limbs, there was a second pair of arms jutting awkwardly from under and behind the first pair. The fur was patchy and the skin underneath was covered in pustules.

She thought of the cage she'd seen. Three bears, but only two were accounted for. Had it escaped, mutated by Nathaniel's experiments? Was this one of its deformed offspring?

Nellie edged back into the operating room. The creature stalked in, sniffing the air, snarling angrily.

The tray of surgical gear was just a few feet away. There were knives and saws. They looked puny when compared to the creature's wicked claws and fangs, but they were all she had. Nellie grabbed the nearest knife. She tried not to think about what it had been used for last. She just hoped it was still sharp.

She couldn't leave Sammy, but how could she get to him? The monster seemed to fill the whole room. Even without the claws it looked strong enough to rip her limb from limb.

It leaped and Nellie dove. It flew over her, smashing against the far wall as she rolled under the operating table. She banged her head on the steel edge as she scrabbled up and yelled as a claw cut the back of her calf. She swung the knife behind her and the creature roared as the blade sliced across its paw.

It tore the table out of the floor, ripping it loose from its bolts.

Nellie clutched the knife with both hands and stabbed into the bear's hind legs. Blood spouted from the wound and then the thing swatted her, hurling her off her feet, the knife still stuck in its leg.

Now weaponless, stunned, and head spinning, Nellie crouched as the table smashed against the wall, just inches above her head. All it needed was to hit her once and she was gone.

She needed to get out.

Having ducked the creature twice, she was back in the corridor and beside Sammy. She choked down the fright at the long tears across his back. "Sammy?"

He groaned. Thank God he was still alive.

But for how long?

The monster howled.

"The door . . ." muttered Sammy. "Trap it . . ."

It was their only way out, but right now that didn't matter. Nellie lowered Sammy up against the wall and ran over to the door. There was a control panel, a big rusty box with buttons and dull, unlit bulbs. Cables hung loose from the dented cover and there was an abandoned mouse nest in among the wiring.

"Red to red," said Sammy, his eyes struggling to stay focused. He was losing consciousness by the second. "Blue to blue."

"Red to red. Blue to blue. Got it."

But it was dark. Was that red, or was that brown? And in the dim light the green and blue looked the same.

The creature was smashing up the operating room. Perhaps it thought she was hiding in there, or maybe it was just filled with so much hate it just wanted to destroy everything.

Sparks jumped as she wound together what she guessed were the red wires. Somewhere within the door, mechanisms and cogs came to life. Rusty pistons began to slide, awakened after almost fifty years.

The monster heard. There was a loud crash as it smashed one last thing. Then it sprang toward the source of the noise.

"Blue to blue, blue to blue, blue to blue . . ." Nellie repeated it like a prayer. Her fingers were slippery with sweat, and she wasn't sure it was blue to blue but she began knotting the copper wiring together.

The monster raced toward her, howling with madness. It stretched out its arms . . .

The control panel burst into flame as Nellie dove away.

The pistons screamed as the emergency door slammed down.

Nellie hugged Sammy, eyes squeezed shut, expecting a sudden blow from the deadly claws. The creature roared and screamed, and she heard the claws tear against metal.

Why wasn't she dead?

The thing was right next to her.

She opened her eyes.

The door had come down, but not quickly enough. It had caught the monster halfway, trapping it so it had its forelegs and shoulders on one side, the hindquarters on the other. It flailed wildly, less than a foot from them.

And yet the door continued to grind, trying to close.

The creature was being steadily crushed.

It hissed. Each breath became a more desperate gasp than the last. The door was squeezing its lungs, slowly suffocating it. It beat its paws feebly against the door.

It stared at Nellie; it was a look she'd never forget. The fury gave way to fear. Then its eyes closed and the monster's body slumped and it let out a soft sigh.

"It's dead," Nellie said. She came over to Sammy and peeled back his torn jacket. She bit her lip. There were three deep tears, each about six inches long. "I need to get you to a hospital, right now." She emptied out her backpack and opened up the first-aid kit. "I'll patch you up. The moment we get a signal, we'll call for help. You have insurance?"

"Don't make jokes. Laughing hurts." Sammy wiped the sweat from his face and grinned, though it was bordering on a grimace. "Now, if you don't mind, I think I'm going to faint."

CHAPTER 27

Location Unknown

Dan had woken up a few hours ago in a room that was just this side of a cell. No windows, air coming in through ducts, the strange smell of a place newly built, all drying paint and dust. The meal had been basic, but enough to get some strength back into his groggy body.

Then, he had no idea how much later, guards came in and pushed him out.

"The boss wants a word," one of them declared.

The construction was steel, glass, and concrete—and massive. Pipes ran along the ceiling, huge with warning symbols and chemical codes. The inhabitants ranged from guards to laboratory technicians to more guards. They came loaded with pistols and submachine guns and an attitude of "shoot a lot first, then ask questions much, much later."

"Wow," Dan said. "Early Bond villain architecture. I bet you've got a giant laser beam here, don't you?"

They didn't lead Dan to a laser beam, but instead, to an arboretum.

Outside the gigantic glass dome lay snow and mountains and endless storm clouds. Within were towering palm trees, wide oaks, tropical fruit trees, and a sea of flowers, all growing randomly among the trunks and drooping branches.

Nathaniel Hartford was pruning the rosebushes. His bright shears had already left a pile of dead flower heads on the floor.

The guards kept a discreet distance, but matched his and the Outcast's progress footstep by footstep. One snap of Nathaniel's fingers and Dan would have five burly armed men sitting on top of him.

Nathaniel paused as Dan approached. His eyes were a watery blue, but Dan was fixed by his gaze.

"Let's have a good look at you," ordered the Outcast.

Grandfather and grandson faced each other.

"Ah, there is more Hope in you than there is in your sister," said Nathaniel. "Amy is much more like her grandmother. Strange, don't you think?"

"No, not really."

He's just an old man.

Liver spots decorated the backs of his wrinkled hands. He stooped slightly, and the firmness had long gone from his face, leaving sagging skin and sharp cheekbones.

Dan stared at him, trying to see how much of his

grandfather he might recognize, not just in himself and Amy, but in the old photographs of his mother.

What had father and daughter shared? He caught glimpses of her in the old man's face, brief and slight, yet there she was in his gaze, in the way he held his hands, in the still poise.

A hard, bitter emotion caught in his throat. Two opposite urges tugged within his chest. This was his grandfather. Apart from Amy, this man was the closest living relative Dan had. Yet this was his enemy, who was dedicated to destroying the Cahills.

Dan forced his gaze away from the Outcast. He didn't trust himself. "Where am I?"

"I call it the Hive, Dan," said Nathaniel.

The name fit. The panels looked like sections of honeycomb, and bees drifted through the sweaty air, searching the flowers.

"I've always been an engineer at heart. I love building things. And tinkering. I always needed to know how things worked." Nathaniel looked around his construction. "Do you know my first job was on the Manhattan Project?"

Dan stopped dead. "You helped build the atomic bomb?"

Nathaniel waved his hand dismissively. "Oh, I was a mere number cruncher. But it was I who sized the detonators within Little Boy, the nuclear bomb dropped on Hiroshima on August 6, 1945. You know how an atomic bomb works, I presume? Or is your knowledge of science and history as backward as I fear?"

Dan scowled. "The bomb had two sections of uranium. Separate, they were safe, but together, they reached a critical mass and caused an atomic explosion."

"Exactly." Nathaniel smiled at Dan like a benevolent grandfather. "A projectile, fired into a target. I sized the bags of cordite that shot one into the other. Isn't it curious how such a simple ingredient can change the world?" He looked sideways at Dan. "Sound familiar?"

"The Cahill serum," said Dan. "Is this a test, Nat? Or can we just get to the point? You want to re-create the serum, we know that."

"Hardly," said the Outcast. "I want to destroy it. Once and for all."

"I'm the only one who knows the formula. Why didn't you just have Melinda shoot me? Problem solved. Why show me all this?"

"Killing you would only be a temporary measure. What would prevent some clever chap, or girl, in the future, from uncovering the formula for themselves? The genie is out of the bottle. Once you know it's possible, others will try and achieve the same thing. Look at how many countries developed atomic and nuclear technology after we did. No, I want a more permanent, everlasting solution."

"How?"

"By taking that formula out of your head."

"To do what with it? Use it on yourself?"

Nathaniel shook his head. "No. I will corrupt it. Turn it into the very opposite of what it is. Into the most perfect poison. But one with a single purpose." He turned slowly and pointed the blades of his shears at Dan's neck.

Dan shifted a pace back. "Which is what?"

Nathaniel gazed at him coldly. "To wipe out the Cahill bloodline forever."

CHAPTER 28

Dan spoke. "That's impossible. There must be thousands of us; descendants of Gideon and Olivia Cahill must be spread all over the world by now. You'd need an army, thousands of people, and even then, it would take decades to find everyone."

Nathaniel scoffed. "People? Who said anything about people? And I have not thousands, but hundreds of thousands. And my army will have all the time in the world. They'll carry on their duty, generation after generation. No matter how long it takes, the Cahills will be removed from this world."

He had to be lying. Nothing he was saying made any sense. Dan continued. "Even if you did make this supertoxin of yours, how would you get it to target the right people?"

"By creating a toxin that affects only those with a specific DNA makeup. In this case, the Cahill gene. It's taken many years and countless millions of dollars to decode the unique DNA of Gideon and Olivia, the gene that all the branches have in common. Fortunately, I've had the time and the fortune to do it. And I am that close to making it happen."

He tapped Dan's forehead. "I just need the formula."

"You really think I'm going to tell you?"

"Oh, yes." Nathaniel smiled coldly. "One way or another."

Dan said nothing. He needed to stall, maybe a day, maybe two. Sooner or later—

Nathaniel laughed. "Ah, I see. You want to play for time in the hope of escape, or rescue?"

Nathaniel took the shears to a fresh bush. "I've studied your escapades, as any proud grandfather would do. I've seen how perfectly you and Amy work together. Wherever there's one, the other won't be far behind. So you believe, quite naturally, your older sister will arrive soon and save you."

Snip, snip. Two heads tumbled.

"Not this time, Dan."

"What do you mean?"

"I mean I know she's in China, with two of your friends."

Dan's blood ran cold.

"I thought it would take longer to find her, but today seems to be my lucky day. Alek Spasky reported to me a few hours ago that your sister had arrived at the symposium. He's waiting for her and I'm expecting his call any minute now." Nathaniel gestured to one of the guards.

The guard nodded and handed over a cell phone.

Nathaniel flicked the screen on. "The wonders of modern technology." He handed it over to Dan.

Dan took it and stared at the screen. The image was blurred and the sound crackled.

Nathaniel stood at his shoulder. "I need you to understand one thing very clearly. There is no hope."

The image began to clear, and a face, a familiar face, came into focus.

"Amy?" Dan's blood ran cold.

"Dan! Dan! Can you hear me?"

Dan gripped the cell phone, squeezing it so hard that the plastic creaked. "Amy! I'm here!"

He shook it. He could hardly see her: the screen was a blizzard of static, his sister's face a frightened mask.

Her voice crackled through the speakers. "I—I don't have much time, Dan. You have to listen. . . ."

"Where are you? Tell me!"

Amy sighed. Her shoulders slumped and she seemed to crumble from inside. He'd never seen her so small, so beaten.

How could she be? She was his sister. They'd been through everything together and had always come out on top.

Always.

CHAPTER 29

Nathaniel stood over Dan, wondering what turmoil of emotions the boy must be feeling right now. It had been so easy to break him.

Family could be both a weakness and a strength. Grace had taught him that.

Now a little more of a push and Dan would crumble entirely.

A deep animal growl rose from Dan's throat. Nathaniel stepped back and gave his men the nod. Dan had just seen his sister killed; he was about to—

Dan exploded. The guards—the best money could buy—were taken by surprise. Dan rammed his knee deep into the gut of the guy in front and his elbow into the face behind him. A third tried to grab him but had his fingers bitten to the bone.

He's gone wild!

Nathaniel pushed a guard ahead of him as Dan swung around, his eyes blazing.

The guard raised his machine gun.

"No!" Nathaniel yelled. "I need him alive!"

The guard hesitated; Dan leaped at him and both tumbled into the thick foliage. There was a thud—the sound a head makes when hit by wood—then the leaves of the bushes shook.

"Go grab him!"

The guards gathered themselves quickly. One saw Dan dart from behind a tree trunk.

They fanned out to catch him.

Nathaniel gazed at the blank screen of the cell phone. The bombs he'd had planted within the Shanghai reactor would have gone off by now. In ten minutes or so the coolant waters would reach a critical pressure and cause the reactor to explode. It wouldn't be on a nuclear scale, but he estimated several city blocks would blow with the initial blast.

And he'd be rid of Alek Spasky. The Russian had become a liability. Nathaniel had never been able to control him, not like the others, and such a man had to be handled very carefully, and removed once his usefulness was at an end.

The rest of his allies he'd deal with at Attleboro.

Nathaniel heard Dan shout, and there were sounds of a struggle, then a crash, and after, just weary huffing. Moments later, two guards emerged from the trees, dragging a semiconscious Dan between them. One of the guards had a black eye and another was missing a tooth.

Nathaniel admired that. Was that inherited from Grace's stubbornness or Nathaniel's own determination? The boy would defy him to the very end, that much was obvious.

Nathaniel took hold of Dan's hair and raised his head. "I have wasted enough time with you. I need the thirty-ninth clue. I need the formula."

Dan spat at him.

Nathaniel struggled to hold on to his temper. Why did he hate the boy and girl so much? They were his grandchildren.

No, they are Grace's.

They both embodied so much of her and so little of him. Their parents had died when they were young, so the only true parent had been Grace. What had it been like, in her shadow? For Nathaniel it had meant being permanently left in the dark. Grace had ruled and ruled alone.

He often wondered how she'd ordered his death, back in 1967. Had she lain awake at night, conflicted? Or had it merely been an entry on her daily agenda?

Item 13. Pick up laundry.

Item 14. Kill my husband.

Item 15. Attend opera.

He'd loved her, hated her, but always admired her.

There was a strong family resemblance, so strong that, it seemed to Nathaniel, it had wiped out all traces of him. Grace had left her mark deeper than their skins—she'd marked their souls.

Nathaniel pulled harder, enough to make Dan wince. He smiled. Old, fond memories flooded back. Perhaps this was the best way. . . .

"I was in Germany during the Cold War. That was a war of spies and nowhere was it fought harder than in Berlin. It was a golden age of espionage and there was a great demand for reliable truth serums." He glanced at a pair of steel doors just a few yards away. "No matter how strong you think you are, you will break and tell me everything. Everyone does in the end."

CHAPTER 30

Shanghai, China

Whatever the evacuation plan had been, it had fallen apart with the first siren. No one seemed to know which way to run. Amy helped one man back to his feet after he'd been hurled over by a screaming security guard.

"What's happening?" she asked him.

The man tried to pull away, but she wasn't letting go until she had answers. "The reactor's overheating! The chamber's starting to rupture! We have got to get out of here!"

"Overheating? How?"

The man squirmed. "Please, let me go!"

"Tell me!"

He looked around for help, but it was every man for himself. "Excessive heat buildup. That's usually absorbed by running water as a coolant through the system. But somehow the pumps have failed, so there's no water flow and no way of getting rid of the heat!"

"Failed? How have they failed? What about backups?"

"Please! I don't know! All I know is the reactor temperatures are off the scale!"

Amy released him and the man fled.

This is Nathaniel's disaster replay. What had happened at Chernobyl? The same thing. There had been a spike in energy generated in one of the reactors, but the coolant flow had been too little and too slow to get rid of it. The buildup had caused the explosion.

She needed to get to the control room.

There was a map on the wall and Alek ripped it off. The security doors had all opened, so there was no stopping her from accessing wherever she wanted.

Amy and Alek, dragging Dr. Lin, ran up a steel staircase into a corridor with a large internal window panel. On the other side were control decks and a large electronic schematic of the power station, lit up like a Christmas tree. Bulbs flashed red on all points.

The room was empty. Chairs had been tipped over and there were a few tablets and other electronic devices abandoned on the floor. When the alarm had sounded, they'd left without grabbing anything.

Amy ran up to the deck. The screens pulsed.

All the dials and controls were in Chinese.

She couldn't hear herself think! The alarms were deafening!

This is hopeless. It's going to blow!

Dr. Lin scanned the display board. Alarms dazzled and flashed—the whole system was in catastrophe mode. None of it made any sense to Amy; she felt useless.

The panic swelled in her. She fought down the urge, the almost overwhelming urge, to flee. To run and run and not look back.

A tremor shook the complex. Amy gulped, fearing this was the moment the reactor would explode. The steel beams ground against the concrete as the power station shifted.

Amy turned to Dr. Lin. "What's happening? What went wrong?"

Tears were streaming down Dr. Lin's face. "I—I can't tell. It's all . . ."

"There has to be something!" Amy snapped. "Nathaniel couldn't have sabotaged the entire system! Someone would have noticed!"

Alek approached the wall. "She's right. It would be something relatively small, easily missed."

The wall itself was over twenty feet wide and a dozen high. One huge digital screen filled with the schematic of the fusion reactor. On top of that was a 3-D holographic display, projecting sensor readings. She could decipher some. Temperatures. Flow rates. Pressures. All tripping into the red zone.

The room shook with a second explosion. The floor cracked, and Amy heard a threatening roar from deep within the bowels of the power station.

The display crackled and a panel went blank.

Dr. Lin couldn't stop shaking. "It's too late . . . it's too late."

Amy dragged the doctor to the wall. "You have to tell me what's wrong!"

They faced each other. Amy took a deep breath. Attacking Dr. Lin would do no good. She needed her. "How does the reactor work? Just explain it to me. Simply."

Dr. Lin straightened. She was going into lecture mode. "The reactor is basically a heat generator. In its simplest form it's nothing more than a steam engine. The heat from the reactor heats the water that turns the turbine, which generates the electricity that is then transmitted throughout the city." She pointed to a complex series of lines weaving in and across the schematic. "Here is the generator. There are the flow pipes. Water going in, and water going out, heated to extreme temperatures. It expands to steam, it drives the turbines."

The station rumbled and the display flickered. They didn't have long.

Dr. Lin raised her head and listened. "The pressure is building somewhere. There must be a blockage." She adjusted her glasses and busied herself over the console. "We've got a heat buildup reaching catastrophic levels. That's the problem." She gasped and stabbed her finger at a gate symbol. "One of the coolant valves is jammed shut. That's what's going wrong. And the backup's been taken off line. Who would do that?"

Alek joined them. "Can you switch it on?"

Dr. Lin grimaced. "With the temperature buildup we need both valves open. I can open the backup from here but it won't bleed off the heat quickly enough." She darted to the control desk. "The valve needs to be opened." She clicked on the keyboard. "There are microcameras within the pipes, all used as part of the maintenance program."

One of the panels transformed into a screen, viewing the inside of a pipe. Bubbles distorted the image and the camera had been twisted out of position, but there was a circular steel gate, mostly closed. The coolant frothed and whirled as it tried to get through the small gap between gate edge and the valve frame.

"How do we open it?" Alek asked.

"It has to be done by hand." Dr. Lin shook her head. "It's suicide. You'd have to enter the flow pipes themselves. The pipes pass through the reactor, so the coolant itself is radioactive."

Alek looked from her to the display. "How long would you have before getting a lethal dose?"

Dr. Lin stared. "You cannot be serious."

"How long?"

Dr. Lin brushed her hair from her face. Her lips moved silently as she scanned the readings. "The coolant is absorbing radiation, so you'll need to move fast before they build to fatal levels. The suits have radiation counters on them. Get out before they light all the way through red." Dr. Lin glanced at the display. "Which gives you about ten minutes, given the rate of contamination."

Ten minutes to do such a simple thing. All she had to do was turn a bit of steel, push it open, and they'd save a city. Amy stared at the screen, trying to guess how heavy it might be.

Just put your feet against one side and push. The water pressure will do the rest.

Don't think about the radiation seeping into your bones.

"I've got to get into the flow pipe," Amy said.

"You're insane." Dr. Lin sank into the chair, a look of disbelief still covering her face. "And you can't do it alone. The gate needs to be locked into position, otherwise it'll just slam shut again."

Alek met Amy's gaze.

His wife had died in a reactor. Amy wondered if Natalia thought she'd been a hero, or a fool. She'd saved thousands of lives, but had her death changed Alek? What sort of man would he have been if she'd lived?

Alek smiled. "I am an assassin, not a mass murderer. I'll help."

Dr. Lin donned an abandoned headset. "Take the elevator to level minus six. That's the maintenance level. Go to access hatch sixty-three. There should be a set of full breathing gear, comms, and sealed suits that will offer some protection. The maintenance men use them, but they're prototypes. No one's tested them against anything above five hundred. Make sure you seal them properly. Any gap will mean contamination. Got it?"

Amy cupped her hand around the hologram of the gate. "And when I get to the gate?"

"Get it open as fully as you can. Then get out."

CHAPTER 31

They rushed down to the maintenance room. The whole complex was shaking now, and the walls bent and cracked under the strain. Amy's heart raced like it had never done before. The whole reactor could blow any second.

Alek pushed open the steel door and in they went. The emergency lights filled the room with an eerie red glow, and goose bumps crept along Amy's flesh, despite the stagnant heat that was building.

The sealed suits were folded up neatly within transparent plastic containers. Amy knocked the lid open.

Alongside the suits were small air tanks, breathing apparatus, and a chunky wristband with a digital reader. Nice and simple, with a row of twelve bars, green to orange to red.

"Radiation counters?" Amy guessed.

Alek handed her a headset. He hooked his around his ear and wrapped the throat mic around his neck. "Dr. Lin? Do you hear me?"

"Yes. Are you ready?"

Amy put on her headset and spoke to the waiting scientist as she suited up. "Where do we go now?"

"Through the maintenance door. You'll come up to a pressure hatch. Once you're in that, hit the flood button. That will equalize the pressure on both sides, the side you're in and the pipe. Open up the second hatch at your feet and swim twenty meters to your left. You'll see the jammed valve gate."

"Got it," replied Amy.

Alek and Amy checked each other to make sure their suits were fully sealed. The mask covered the entire face and included a headlight, allowing them to see each other clearly and talk through their comm sets. Amy just hoped she didn't look as terrified as she felt.

Alek tested his mic. "Can you hear me?"

"Loud and clear."

They walked to the hatch and together wound it open. Below was a steel tube, about five feet wide. A short ladder led them down four meters to a second hatch in the floor and a big red toadstool-shaped button on the wall.

Amy waited there while Alek reclosed the hatch above them. It was dark except for the light coming from their headlights.

Alek joined her. He tapped the radiation counter on his forearm. "We won't have long."

Three green bars glowed out of the twelve. A quarter of their time was already gone.

We can do this. In and out.

Amy punched the FLOOD button. Jets of water shot in at their ankles, rising to their knees in a couple of seconds, to their waist in a few seconds more.

Amy slowed down her breathing. She'd done enough scuba diving to know that slow, deep breaths were the best way to conserve oxygen and prevent carbon dioxide from getting trapped in her lungs. Bubbles swirled around her and the water roared, deep and thunderous.

The pipe filled and they both worked at turning the wheel lock on the hatch below them. The steel groaned as it opened, and Alek dropped down first.

Amy checked her reader. The fifth bar was flashing. It was all happening faster than she'd expected.

Could they fix the valve and be back up in time?

She didn't know.

Amy gritted her teeth and descended.

The water surge almost knocked her off her feet, but Alek grabbed her wrist and they both hung on to the lip of the connection and scanned ahead.

"Twenty yards to the left," said Amy. "See anything?"

Alek shook his head. "Too murky." His voice crackled in Amy's earpiece.

The coolant water had a sickly greenish tinge and was filled with bubbles, reducing visibility down to only five or six yards.

The water was dragging them toward the blockage valve, so they used the flow to their advantage.

But as Amy glided along the five-foot-wide pipe, the whole thing shook, and the metal groaned and buckled. Kinks appeared in the steel surface, and the weak spots, the joints between pipe sections, were giving way.

"Watch out," Amy warned. She braced herself against the wall. "Look ahead."

They had reached the broken valve.

The gate valve was simply a circular steel plate, damaged by the sabotage, that was hinged along its center. The plate controlled flow, opening and shutting depending on the needs of the system. But the system needed it open right now, to help reduce the temperature buildup in the core. Now only a sliver of the edge had turned, forcing the water to tear through that gap at high velocity.

Three feet in front of the plate, fixed to a control mechanism in the side of the pipe, was a steel rod. It had been bent out of shape and needed to be eased back into position if the plate was to be opened, and kept open.

"I'll push the plate, you move the rod," said Alek. He tapped his reader. "And we need to be quick."

Half the bars were glowing. They were heading into the red zone.

Amy's headset crackled and Dr. Lin came on. "The pressure in the reactor core has hit a hundred and fifty percent. The shielding's going to rupture if you don't get that flow going right now."

Amy gripped the rod. "Ready!"

Alek pushed the side of the plate, forcing it to turn on its axis. The steel didn't want to move—the explosion had shifted it out of position and its edge was twisted, jagged metal.

The first red bar started flashing. They were into the last two minutes.

Amy pulled, feeling the rod shift ever so slightly.

But if it was going to move a little, she could make it move the whole way.

"On the count of three, Alek!" she shouted. She braced herself against the side of the pipe wall, spreading her feet out to avoid being swept away. "One! Two!" She flexed her fingers and got the best grip she could. "Three!"

Alek roared as he pushed and Amy heaved at the rod, pulling until her arms trembled with pain. "Come . . . on . . ."

The water flow increased as the gate began to open. It pushed Amy, trying to drag her down the pipe. The rod was sliding back into the locking mechanism. Only another few inches . . .

Amy fell forward as the rod slipped back into place. The water gushed over her but she held on even as her feet were lifted up from under her so she dangled like a fish on a line.

"You've done it!" yelled Dr. Lin. "Now hurry back and get out!"

"Come on, Alek!" shouted Amy, more relieved than she'd ever been.

"Cahill . . ."

Amy turned.

Alek was hanging on to the edge of the plate, now fully open. He was slipping in the high flow. Amy's headlight caught the hard grimace on his face as he clung on.

Amy reached out, one hand hanging on to the rod, the other stretched out toward Alek. "Grab it!"

She saw the bars on his arm. Nine flashed.

"Just get out!" he yelled.

"Give me your hand!"

He snarled, and Amy saw his arms quiver with the strain. Then his palm slapped into hers and they locked fingers.

Together, weights combined, they crawled against the flow, heads bowed as the water beat upon them.

Dr. Lin's voice broke through on Amy's headset. "There's an emergency hatch another six feet ahead."

Amy peered forward and saw the circular panel. Too tired to speak, she dragged herself to it and twisted the steel plate open.

CHAPTER 32

The maintenance hatch fell open and the water rushed out of this fresh hole. The pair of them tumbled out, and Amy crashed onto bare concrete, gasping with total exhaustion.

They were in a second maintenance room, smaller, with a watertight door ahead. With body-shaking relief, Amy closed the door behind them.

She sank down, resting her head on her knees, and began trembling. Uncontrollably.

The alarm on her reader continued beeping, but it sounded far away; all she heard was her blood pounding in her ears, her heart throbbing within her wall of ribs.

The fear consumed her; the terror she'd been fighting now rose up and swamped her, body and soul.

How could anyone have planned something so evil?

Alek groaned and blinked. He pulled off his mask and looked around, dazed. He frowned. "You saved me? Why?"

Amy laughed weakly. "I must have had a reason, but I can't think of it right now."

Alek stood up, but Amy spotted the twist of agony. He peeled off his sealed suit.

Amy stopped him. "What's that?"

The sleeve was torn and blood dripped from a tear along Alek's arm. He looked at it and dismissed it. "I must have caught it on the edge of the plate. It's nothing."

"That's not nothing. Dr. Lin warned us about the suits. They were the only things protecting—"

"It's nothing," Alek insisted. "You have my thanks, and for that I give you a parting gift. I know what Nathaniel is planning next."

Amy's eyes widened. "It's not over?"

"Go to Attleboro. He has invited all his allies there to celebrate his victory, to reestablish the Cahill organization, to decide its future. I was asked to attend. He said he had a reward for us."

Amy's mind raced. "I'm guessing it's not flowers and candy."

Alek smiled. "No. Now I suspect he intends to kill us all."

"A final double cross."

So Nathaniel didn't just want to destroy his rivals—he intended to destroy his allies, too. She thought about Vikram, Magnus, Melinda, and the others who'd all thrown their lot in with the Outcast, hoping for a piece of his empire, never realizing he wanted to rule *alone*.

"When's this gathering?" she asked, her thumb on her cell keyboard.

"Two days from now."

Ian and Cara. They were the closest. If they were in Kiev today, a twelve-hour flight and some traveling would get them to Attleboro the day of the assassination. It would be close, but she wasn't going to let Nathaniel commit mass murder, even on her enemies.

Amy didn't move. "What are you going to do?"

Alek gazed at his hands. He balled them into fists. "Go visit Nathaniel Hartford."

That sounded as if it was going to end violently, for him or Nathaniel.

"Take me with you. He has Dan."

Alek scowled. "I do not chaperone children. And my business with Nathaniel promises to be bloody. Now go before I change my mind."

Amy stubbornly stayed exactly where she was. "Take me with you. You need me."

Alek arched an eyebrow. "Oh, and how do you imagine you might be of any help to me?"

"You needed me in that pipe."

Alek looked at her as if he was measuring her will to do what was necessary. "Very well. We need to move quickly, and we have a long way to go. I have some old friends within the Chinese government. They can arrange transportation for us."

"But what about my friends? Jonah and Ham?"

"The Tomas I shot?"

Amy froze.

Alek Spasky was a cold-blooded killer. He showed no remorse at having almost killed Ham. No embarrassment.

Then again, Grace had done similar things, hadn't she? She'd ordered deaths, then still had time for tea afterward. Amy thought back to birthday parties her grandmother had thrown for her and her brother. Then the long silent times when she'd be in her study, door closed and talking in whispers. Ruling the Cahills and being their silver-haired grandmother.

Was Alek really any different?

Was he just another creation of the Cahills? An unpleasant necessity?

He wants revenge on Nathaniel. And I'm just playing along.

"Where are we going?" Amy asked.

"Alaska. Nathaniel has built a new research facility there."

Amy's heart skipped a beat. "What sort of facility?"

"You are afraid for your brother?"

Amy could only nod. Fear had taken her voice.

Alek's face was grim. "You should be."

CHAPTER 33

Attleboro, Massachusetts
Two days later

"I cannot believe we're doing this," said Cara. "Tell me again, why are we doing this?"

Ian shrugged. "Because we're the good guys?"

"Good guys saving bad guys?"

"And through our actions these bad guys may see the error of their ways, give up their lives of villainy, and return to the side of the angels."

"You really believe that?" asked Cara.

"No, not in the slightest. I personally hope my father ends up in a very deep, dark dungeon for the rest of his life."

Ian rocked back on his heels. From their hiding place in the orchard they had a good view of the front of the Cahill mansion.

He ached from too much traveling and not enough resting. That flight out of Kiev in the cargo plane was not something he ever wanted to repeat, and the only bonus was having proper alone-time with Cara. But she'd been all business, wanting to review the information gathered from Amy in Shanghai, and Sammy and Nellie from the Black Forest.

It had been overwhelming, and they'd needed the whole flight to make sense of it and plan their next step. Which was to follow the lead given to them by Alek Spasky, who'd warned them that Nathaniel was planning to kill off all his allies tonight, at the celebratory party in Attleboro.

Ian raised the binoculars and searched the grounds.

It had changed. Nathaniel had removed the topiary along the drive, changed the two nymphs on the fountain to sea snakes, and put up a green-house. Of the changes, the greenhouse was the only one Ian approved of. The design reminded him of Kew Gardens. "Those beehives are new," he said, pointing at six domes on the edge of the lawn. "Nathaniel must love fresh honey."

"Looks like the Outcast is throwing a party," said Cara. "Check out the size of that tent."

"Nathaniel has reasons to be happy." Ian scanned the three catering vans. Waiters were transferring silver dishes back and forth to the tent and trolleys of champagne and dessert into the greenhouse. "Unless I'm mistaken, he's even imported truffles from Salzburg." He sniffed the air again. "No, I'm wrong. . . ."

"No one can smell truffles from here."

"Not Salzburg. Alpbach," Ian concluded. He'd learned to ski there. Back in better days. He pointed at the rearmost van, the one with the snowflake logo. "And that lorry has come all the way from Alaska. Look at the license plate."

"Livia's Sorbet Company? Nathaniel's spent a lot of money on just a few tubs of ice cream."

"It rings a vague bell," said Ian, frowning. "It must be very special. I remember once having tea with the Duke of Brixtonshire and tasting the most delightful jam. I asked him—"

She was giving him the look, so Ian decided to hold off explaining the paradise that was to be found in a spoon of that particular jam. It was, incidentally, his father's favorite, too. Nathaniel had a sly sense of humor, giving the condemned man his favorite meal before his execution.

Tires on the gravel behind forced them to crouch lower. A limousine rolled past, its windows tinted and the license plate English.

Ian's blood ran cold.

The limo parked by the entrance to what had been, until very recently, Ian's home.

Vikram Kabra opened his own door and emerged. He paused to gaze about him, as though a lord inspecting his new domain.

"Greedy as ever," muttered Ian. "How many homes do you have already?"

Cara held Ian's hand, and the hot rage that had been rising, almost unnoticed, began to cool.

Vikram adjusted his bow tie and buttoned his dinner jacket. Still, he lingered.

"He's measuring the windows for new curtains," said Ian. "He's thinking the same thing as all the others."

"That once Nathaniel's gone, they'll take command of the Cahills."

"Exactly." Ian shook his head. "They don't understand Nathaniel at all."

But the clues had been there all along. One after the other, Nathaniel had worked toward destroying each of the branches of the Cahills. It was only logical, in a twisted kind of way, that he'd want to destroy his allies, too.

"We can't just march in there and tell everyone that Nathaniel plans to kill them," said Cara.

"No. We need to find out what the Outcast's move will be. Neutralize it and use it as proof. That'll get them . . . on our side." He took off his jacket and folded it neatly. "Come on. We need to get inside." Ian stood up and held out his hand. "Follow me."

Cara stood up beside him. She took his hand. "Don't you know it."

CHAPTER 34

They waited for the waiter to leave the catering van before they dashed the ten yards from the edge of the trees to the back of the van. A quick jump and they were in. They rummaged around until Cara held up a white waiter's jacket. "This should fit you." She tossed it over and found one for herself.

She put it on. Ian smiled approvingly. Cara looked pretty great in anything.

"What's to stop them from noticing us?" she said as she tucked her hair into a cap.

"We're not going to serve at the table, and given what snobs my father and the rest of them are, it's beneath them to notice the hired help."

They jumped out of the van. Ian checked his watch. "They'll be serving in about fifteen minutes. They'll be having predinner cocktails right now, probably on the southern terrace. That'll give us time to check the front half of the mansion."

Cara grabbed a spare tray and handed Ian an empty crystal jug. "We need to look like we're busy doing something," she said. They walked to the front entrance. Cara paused to take a deep breath. "Better put your game face on."

"The trouble is my game is test cricket," said Ian. "That's usually played over five days with breaks for tea."

Cara shook her head. "Then I'd better go first."

The two guards at the door nodded them in. They'd watched waiters go in and out all evening; these two barely registered. It was all going according to plan.

They were in the hallway. Ian pointed up the sweeping staircase. "We'll start up top and work our way down. I'll take the west—"

"You there!" A man emerged from the side door, the one that led into the kitchens. "I asked for four crates of Bollinger and there are only three! Go speak—"

Ian blinked at the man. It was Mr. Berman, his ex-butler. The trouble was that while snobs might not notice the servants, the servants themselves noticed the servants.

Mr. Berman blinked, his jaw working up and down. Then his voice returned. "Ian . . . Kabra . . . ?"

"Uh-oh," said Cara.

Berman stumbled away, took a deep breath, and shouted. "Ian Kabra!"

CHAPTER 35

Cara slammed her tray into Berman's face with a deafening clang. Ian caught him as he collapsed.

The two guards burst in, pistols out. "Don't move!"

Ian whimpered. "The poor man fainted!"

The guard kept his weapon steady and aimed at Ian's forehead. "We heard something. A bang. What was that?"

"Er . . ." Ian glanced about. He wasn't good at this bluffing thing. "Er . . ."

"It was the dinner gong," said Cara. She held up the padded club next to the copper gong standing beside the staircase. "Sorry, I couldn't resist."

"Yes . . . I think the shock of someone other than him hitting it was too much," said Ian. "Mr. Berman takes that sort of thing very seriously. You know what butlers are like."

They didn't, so they were willing to believe. The guard scanned the hallway once more, couldn't see any obvious threats, and reholstered his firearm. "What are you going to do with him?"

Ian nodded to a side door. "There's a couch in the library."

Cara grabbed the butler's legs as the guards returned to their posts.

"Come on," said Ian, holding Berman from under his shoulders. "We want the door on the right."

"That's not the library, Ian."

"No, it's the broom cupboard."

They shoved him in with the mops and buckets, having to bend him double so he'd fit. Ian locked the door. "Now, where were we?"

"Trying to stop Nathaniel from killing everyone. How do you think he'll do it? Use the guards?"

"Not enough of them. Too great a chance someone will escape. I'd suggest a bomb, but Nathaniel won't want the mansion damaged, not right after having spent all this time refurbishing it." Ian tapped a bronze bust that stood beside him in a neat alcove in the hall. "He's even had old Octavian polished."

"Octavian? A family member?"

Ian smiled. Really, sometimes he wondered what exactly kids learned in the American education system. "Hardly. Octavian was the birth name of Augustus Caesar, the first Roman emperor. He was the adopted son—"

"Whatever," snapped Cara. She gazed out the window toward the lawn. "Snipers? There's plenty of places you could hide them. There could be a dozen in that tree right now."

"The glass in the greenhouse is bulletproof. It could take a direct hit from a fifty caliber and still not break."

"How do you know that?"

Ian winced. "I . . . er . . . had it installed. They were doing a discount."

"You're not like other boys, are you?" She snapped her fingers. "The catering! What if he's poisoned one of the dishes? Amy said Alek had warned her that Nathaniel was studying toxins."

Ian paled. "Only the most base, uncouth philistine would even consider spoiling such a dinner." Then he returned his attention to the Roman emperor. "What was that sorbet company called?"

"Livia, I think."

"Livia was the name of Augustus's wife. It's said that he wanted to pass the reins of power to one of his generals, not Livia's son by another marriage, Tiberius."

"So?"

"So she wanted to make sure Tiberius became emperor. She knew Augustus had a fondness for figs. . . ."

Cara winced. "Let me guess, she poisoned the figs?"

"Every single one on his favorite fig tree. Took all night, they say."

Cara smiled. "You thinking what I'm thinking?"

Ian's smile mirrored hers. "The sorbet."

CHAPTER 36

Alaska

Amy gazed down at the vast field of trees. The Alaskan wilderness spread out in all directions. It was as if she'd gone to the edge of the world and left humanity behind.

The thought seized her. To wander into the trees and disappear. She could imagine it—the silence, the peace.

The steady, constant drone of the helicopter made her drowsy. That, and the fact she'd not slept since . . . when? Ages ago.

Getting out had been harder than expected. After the near disaster with the Shanghai reactor, the whole place had been on lockdown. Word must have gotten out it was an act of sabotage, so the government had come down hard, suspecting terrorism.

They'd not been able to risk flying out of Shanghai, so they had paid off a truck driver to smuggle them out of the city, and that had cost them time.

They'd found a small regional airport, then swapped flights in Hong Kong, another frustrating day not knowing what was happening to Dan.

Now Amy was close, but dreaded the lost time, time Dan had been left at the mercy of a man willing to blow up a city.

Please don't let me be too late.

Alek pointed to a ridge ahead. "There's the valley. We'll have to land on this side and cross over on foot if we're to avoid being spotted."

"Just as long as we get Dan."

The helicopter banked to the left and descended, so within a minute they were skimming over the treetops. Alek kept the course pond-smooth, riding the air as lightly as a feather. "There."

It was a clearing, actually a patch of snowy ground beside a frozen river. Amy spotted a couple of outbuildings and a narrow dirt track disappearing into the forest.

"It's an old hunting lodge," said Alek. "No one uses it anymore."

The engine whined as he shifted up a gear and hovered over the center of the clearing. Clouds of snow swirled in the vortex of the rotor blades, but Amy could see Alek was an expert at this. The helicopter touched down with perfect precision.

Amy jumped out the moment the propellers stopped turning, her backpack on one shoulder. She wanted to get a move on.

Alek hopped out. He tossed his own pack into the patchy snow then, with much more care, then removed a second, longer bag.

"What's in here?" Somehow Amy didn't think it was a fishing rod.

Alek unzipped a few inches, revealing the dark steel of a barrel. "It's my sniper rifle. A Mauser SR-93, but I had a gunsmith in Vienna make a few modifications. It's good at—"

"We're not taking it," Amy declared.

"We're here to stop Nathaniel. And a bullet does that *very* effectively."

Yes, Alek was right. Stopping Nathaniel Hartford had to be their priority, even before saving Dan. But it was hard to think like that. How could she separate the needs of the mission, ending the Outcast's madness, with her personal desire to save her brother?

And as bad as Shanghai could have been, she knew that it was not Nathaniel's endgame. There was more to come, worse to come.

"I don't like guns. It makes killing the first option when it should be the last." She waved at his jacket. "And that Walther PPK you have tucked under your armpit can stay here, too."

He glowered, but relented. The pistol came out and he slammed it down on the pilot seat. "Satisfied? Perhaps you should tie both my hands behind my back also?"

How did I end up here? Working with a KGB assassin?

Amy was going to have to review her decision-making process when this was all over. "Let's just get a move on," she said.

Alek frowned as he gazed down the path. "Keep an eye on these trees. Nathaniel may have a patrol out."

Amy turned to search. She couldn't see anything.

Alek picked up his pack, and the pair headed down the path.

The hike was upward. The trees thinned as the route turned into ice and rock. Amy's legs burned as they marched up the steep slope. Despite the cold, she was sweating heavily, and her pack felt twice as heavy as it had at the beginning.

Alek picked the route and Amy slogged behind. There was no talking—what did they have to say to each other? This was a partnership of necessity, not choice. Amy wasn't interested in knowing anything more about him.

Still, she couldn't help but wonder.

This man had loved, once. He'd had a wife and she'd filled his heart.

The Spaskys were a strange family. Cold-hearted killers, yet with a seed of self-sacrifice, even hero-ism, buried deep down. Alek's sister had died saving Amy, and even now Amy didn't understand why.

Alek was carved of hard edges and brutal will. There was no softness in the clifflike angles of his cheeks or joy in the flinty hardness of his gray eyes.

But something was wrong. He was more gaunt that before. The few days they'd traveled together he'd lost weight and his skin, pale anyway, was a jaundiced yellow. And this hike had him wheezing.

"Let me carry that," said Amy, pointing at his backpack. "Just for a while."

Alek glared at her. "I'm fine."

He was anything but fine.

The suit had torn, and he'd been cut while in the radioactive waters. That radiation was now in his blood, killing him from the inside.

How long did he have?

It was dusk and the sky bled red and purple when Alek paused at the top of the ridge. "There."

Amy forced herself up the last few yards.

The ridge now dropped down into a valley. The conifers were as dense as ever, but the bottom of the valley was dominated by a vast geo-dome of shimmering pearl.

"It's called the Hive," said Alek. "That's where we'll find Nathaniel and your brother."

It had to be half a mile in diameter, and there were smaller domes nestled around it. The surface was made of huge hexagonal panels; Amy could see why it had been named the Hive.

There were more basic concrete outbuildings as well as rows of greenhouses.

Alek shoved Amy off her feet.

"Hey!"

He ducked down beside her and put his finger to his lips.

There was nothing, then she saw a figure emerge from the trees, some fifty yards down.

The man wore a heavy parka and winter camo, and carried an assault rifle. There was a pair of binoculars dangling from his neck and in his webbing he carried spare magazines and a walkie-talkie.

He began moving toward them, eyes searching the path ahead.

He's going to see our footprints.

It was dark, but was it dark enough?

The guy looked serious, not some rent-a-goon, but a real professional. The man lowered his rifle and thumbed off the safety.

He pointed it at the bush where Amy was crouching.

CHAPTER 37

"Come out, and hands where I can see them," the man demanded.

Where was Alek? He'd been right next to her.

Amy didn't move.

A three-round burst into the tree beside her jolted her into action. Amy stood, hands raised. "Don't shoot."

"Closer."

"I was out hiking. I got lost. I didn't know this was private property. Look, I'll just turn around and head back."

"Stay exactly where you are." Rifle held with one hand, he reached for his walkie-talkie.

That's when Amy saw Alek. He emerged a yard or two from behind the man and raised a pistol, silencer fixed, to the back of the man's bare head.

"No!" Amy screamed.

The soldier spun, knocking the aim wide. It blew off a piece of bark, inches from Amy's face.

Amy had trained in martial arts, and trained hard.

But she'd never seen anything like this.

Alek dropped his pistol and swept his hand across the man's windpipe, and would have crushed it but for the soldier blocking it with the rifle. He reacted by slamming the butt into Alek's gut.

Alek dropped with a grunt but dragged the man down with him.

Even rolling in the snow, their assault on each other was unrelenting. Knee strikes, elbow slams, even a head butt. The soldier went for a dagger strapped to his thigh, but Alek knotted the rifle strap around his neck.

The man's face reddened. He clawed behind him, trying to tear at Alek's eyes, but Alek steadily tightened the strap.

The struggle stopped and the man went limp.

Alek collapsed into the snow, exhausted.

How long had that taken? Seconds?

Seconds of action, after a lifetime of training.

Alek rolled onto his back, gasping. The fight had exhausted him.

Amy reached out to help him up but he brushed her hand away. "I can get up myself."

"Is he dead?" asked Amy.

"No. Unconscious for a few hours." Alek collected his pistol and the man's submachine gun. Amy saw his hand tremble as he brushed the snow off and inspected it for damage. "Heckler and Koch MP5. That'll do very nicely."

"I said no guns." Alek must have grabbed his pistol when he'd told her to check the trees. The oldest trick in the book and she'd fallen for it.

"You're welcome to try to take it off me."

That sounded like a really bad idea. Amy checked the man in the snow and picked up a pulse. "We'll gag him and tie him up." She took his radio and his security pass.

Alek frisked the man thoroughly, taking his knife and a set of car keys, anything he might use to cut himself free. He swapped his jacket for the man's parka and then tied him up with the shoulder strap of the SMG and gagged him with his own woolen hat.

They walked on and reached the perimeter fence an hour after dark. Floodlights covered the ten yards or so of clear ground from the edge of the trees to the fence itself, some twenty feet high and topped with razor wire.

"We could dig under it," Amy suggested.

"The fence will be buried a meter into the earth to prevent exactly that."

"Then how do we get in?"

Alek smiled. "That all depends on how much you trust me." He lifted the parka hood so it covered his face and pointed the H&K at her.

CHAPTER 38

Alek shoved Amy before him, and she stumbled into the patch of floodlit ground in front of the gate.

There was a small control room on the inside of the gate. A soldier, wearing the same style parka as Alek, walked out with a coffee mug and a flashlight, which he shone at Amy. "What have you got?"

"A stray hiker," said Alek, doing a remarkably good American accent. "Says she got lost looking for the campsite."

"This time of year?" said the soldier, shaking his head. "Stupid kid. Just slot her and dump her in the woods. The wolves will take care of the rest."

Amy gulped. Suddenly, the fear was real. Now would be a perfect time for Alek to betray her.

"She wouldn't have come out here alone," Alek replied. "Let's bring her in and find out where her friends might be."

The soldier hesitated, then nodded to his companion in the control room.

The gates rolled open.

Alek rubbed his hands. "That coffee fresh?"

"Pot's just boiled. Help yourself."

The control room was steam-room hot compared to the outside. Alek poured himself a coffee while Amy stood in the corner, pretending to be too terrified to speak, which wasn't far from the truth.

The room was lit by the glow of six surveillance screens constantly flicking from one camera to another, watching all points along the perimeter. They'd have been spotted the moment they'd tried to get over the fence. Alek's bluff seemed to be working.

"No one else reported finding hikers, have they?" asked Alek. "They might be in lockup already."

The soldier at the screen shook his head. "The only person in lockup is that kid the boss brought in."

Amy's heart jumped. Dan!

The soldier laughed. "But he won't be bothering nobody. Not after what's been done to him."

"What have you done?" Amy grabbed the man and hauled him out of his chair. "What have you done to Dan?"

Alek cursed and smashed his mug into the second man's head. He went down without a fuss.

The man Amy held fumbled for his holster but Amy, rage fueling her, slammed him against the wall, hard enough to rattle his brain. "Tell me!"

Alek held his pistol against the man's temple. "I would. And I'd hurry."

The soldier looked from one to the other, not sure who was the most frightening, the girl with the blazing eyes or the man with the cold ones.

"I'm going to ask you one last time," snarled Amy, her fists quivering with barely suppressed rage. "What have you done with my brother?"

CHAPTER 39

Attleboro, Massachusetts

Tall orchids drooped over the winding path, and there was a bounty of lilies, walls of roses, tulips, and many more exotic flowers. A thick perfume hung over the whole space. Bees worked from one stem to another, weaving through the dense foliage.

There was the chime of glass up ahead, and a few moments later they were in the central courtyard, the only space bare of plants. Wrought-iron tables circled the perimeter and two waiters worked at setting up champagne flutes in preparation for a toast.

Cara nudged him. "Over there. The sorbet."

It was humid, so the sorbets were still in two refrigerated displays. Ian peered through the glass lid. "My word. They've even got a fig-flavored one."

Cara followed the power cable from the cabinet to a socket in the wall. She pulled it out. The sorbets would be sticky puddles within ten minutes. No one would be eating them. "Job done."

"And lives saved. This was certainly easier than trying to stop a nuclear meltdown."

Cara nodded. "Just one thing left to do." She took off the waiter's jacket and threw it into the bushes. "Leave."

"Why the rush? You've just arrived." A voice rose out of the mist ahead of them.

Figures emerged from all around.

Vikram folded his arms as he faced his son. "Gate-crashing parties, Ian? Whatever happened to the good manners I taught you?"

Ian glowered at him. "You taught me nothing 'good,' Father."

Magnus was there, so was Patricia Oh. Behind them, other traitors were lined up, all in their finest evening wear. Their smiles were sinister, ruthless. Pearls glistened, diamonds sparkled, gold shimmered. The women wore Chanel, Dior, Versace. The men's tuxedos came directly from the finest tailors on London's Savile Row.

They were dressed to kill.

"You have to listen to us," said Cara, stepping between Ian and his father. "Nathaniel wants you all dead. That's why he's invited you here."

"Ridiculous," said Magnus. "And desperate. Nathaniel has given us everything we asked for."

"And he's about to take it all away," continued Cara. She gestured to the sorbet. "He was planning to poison you all."

Vikram raised an eyebrow. "The Livia sorbet? Don't be idiotic."

"It's the truth," said Ian. "He wants you all dead.

Only then will his vengeance against the Cahills be complete."

Magnus paused. "There's a simple way to know." He nodded to two men. "Grab the girl."

Ian leaped forward, but Magnus swatted him clean off his feet and he flew across the courtyard.

Cara kicked out, but the two men, both Tomases, were impervious to her attacks. One grabbed her arm and wrenched it behind her, the other clenched her jaw and forced it open.

Ian tried to get to his feet but Cara saw the blood dripping from his head. He stumbled a few feet before collapsing.

Vikram took a bowl. "Fig or lemon?" He smiled, and scooped out some of the lemon. "I do hope it's not too bitter."

Cara struggled. She tried to twist her head away but she was trapped. The man's fingers were as hard as steel clamps.

Vikram stood before her. "So, you are the girl Ian loves? I had no idea he had such poor taste." He pinched her nose. "It would never have worked."

He shoved the sorbet down her throat.

CHAPTER 40

Cara swallowed the sorbet.

It stung, but that's what sorbets did. It tasted . . . delicious.

Vikram sneered. "I have raised a fool." He snapped his fingers. "Lock them up somewhere."

Cara spat out the rest of the sorbet as she was shoved up next to Ian and marched back to the building. "We got it wrong. Maybe Nathaniel wants these guys around after all."

Ian glanced back at the party. "No. He's going to double-cross them, one way or the other, and it's going to be today, when he has them all here."

"Then how?" Cara asked.

Ian shrugged.

The guards led them along the lawn. Cara could still taste the icy lemon sorbet in the back of her throat.

The flower beds on either side were in full bloom. Lilies grew in semiwild patches, there were drooping bluebells, and a rambling rosebush. Butterflies fluttered through the forest of flowers and bees swooped, collecting rich pollen from the treasure trove all about them.

Cara backed away as one buzzed a few inches from her. She hated bees. Wasps. Hornets. She'd been stung once when she was a small kid and had reacted badly. Two days in the hospital badly.

"Bees . . ." she muttered.

"What?" asked Ian.

The guard shoved him forward. "No talking."

Cara gazed around. There were a lot of bees out. She didn't usually see them until next month, when the air warmed and summer truly arrived.

The guards took them into the mansion and up into the attic. Both were pushed through the small hatch and then the door was bolted.

"Lovely," said Ian. "Here with the spiders and dust."

They couldn't stand up straight; the roof pitched sharply and even the apex was just five feet from the floor. Dust motes floated among the old, moldy furniture, but at least there was light coming from a row of small barred windows that looked down onto the driveway on one side and back onto the lawn and the greenhouse on the other.

Ian hunched himself by the window. "Looks like they're starting on the sorbet."

Cara sat down beside him. "You did what you thought was right."

Ian didn't seem in the mood for chat, just for feeling sorry for himself.

Cara peered past him. She trusted Ian, and his judgment. He was a Lucian, but he cared. Maybe that was why it never quite worked out. There were two parts of his soul, always conflicted. The Lucian part was out for himself, but his heart was thinking what was best for the whole.

"I can barely see anything," she complained. "Move over."

"But there are cobwebs."

He caught her look. Ian sighed and drew out his handkerchief, then cleared the cobwebs away from the window frame.

Cara stopped him. "What's that?" She took his hand and opened up the silken cloth.

"A cobweb? With a dead insect?"

A bee. A bee trapped in the web. Dead, for sure, but still very whole. She looked more closely.

"You ever seen markings like this?" she asked.

Ian made a face. "Yuck."

"Look, Ian. Tell me what you see."

The bee's fur was golden, but instead of stripes there was a single patch of black. The patch had a shape. Ian narrowed his eyes. "It looks like . . ."

"A skull," said Cara. "The bee's marked with death."

CHAPTER 41

The Hive, Alaska

Dan lay on the hard tiles. They smelled of sharp, acidic antiseptic. They were cold. Through them he felt the almost subsonic drum of . . . what? Machinery? Engines turning, transformers humming.

He curled up on the floor. He felt detached from his senses, as if his brain and body were working in separate time zones. His head was fuzzy with whatever drug they'd given him.

But one thought turned over and over in his mind.

Amy's dead.

His chest felt hollow, as if his heart were gone.

They had him, as trapped as trapped can be. In a cell. In a hidden valley in a thousand miles of wilderness.

Footsteps beat the corridor outside and Dan grimaced; were they coming for him again? But then the steps moved past the door and away.

They didn't want him now. But they'd come . . .

how many times? Three? Four? He'd been taken to a room with bright lights and a chair and men in white clothes. He tried to work out how much time had passed. A few days, that was for sure, but how many? He couldn't see the sun.

They wanted the formula for the 39 Clues serum. Had he told them?

He couldn't remember.

If he hadn't, then they'd come again, to try to get the secret out of him.

He had to find a way. There might be no escape, but how would he know if he didn't try?

He forced his eyes open. At first he could only see a blur, but then his gaze came back into focus.

He lay in a white cube, maybe seven feet in each direction. There was a door.

A door. And through that door he would find a way out. But he needed to get through that door.

The door.

. . .

. . .

Dan jerked awake. He'd drifted off. He rubbed his face.

Get up. Do something. Don't just lie there.

Okay, I'm getting up.

"And having a conversation with myself. Yep, nice one, Dan." His voice sounded strange, but it was good to hear something. It was a start.

Dan got to his feet. And stumbled.

Whoa. Why is the ground tilting like that?

Dan leaned against the wall and gave himself a minute to find his balance.

Now where am I?

The soft drone of air came from a grille in the ceiling, only four or five inches square. Beside it was a short halogen tube, providing the cold, clear white light. They'd put him in a pair of white pants and a tunic tied at the back. He was barefoot and bare-armed. The arms bore a row of Band-Aids, three on each forearm. That's where the truth serum had gone in.

Escape. Escape. Escape.

What else was in this room?

A pile of bedding. A thin mattress and an even thinner blanket.

He turned the handle; it was locked. But locked how? Bolt or key?

Worse. An electromagnetic lock. There would be a keypad on the other side of the door. Dan rested his ear against it. So that was where the strange humming was coming from.

The deadbolt was tempered steel and set into a steel frame; he'd need a Tomas or two to break it down. He tapped the walls. Concrete. That would be a couple of hours' work with a sledgehammer even if he had full strength.

He spotted an air gap between the bottom of the door and the floor. Dan dropped to his knees and peered through. It was only an inch high but gave him a glimpse of the corridor.

Nothing special. This was just a service corridor lined with storerooms and minor offices. Bare concrete walls given a quick lick of paint. A rush job and unfinished.

Escape. Escape. Escape.

Dan put a foot on the door handle, and fingertips hooked on the doorframe, lifted himself up toward the air grille. It was plastic and easy to knock out. He searched the space above. There was a void of five or six inches, so even if he'd been able to get up there, it was too narrow to crawl along. Fixed to the underside were cable trays, and tied to the trays were bundles of power cables, communications wiring, and the red-cased alarm cables.

Escape. Escape. Escape.

He dropped to the floor before his arms gave out.

That humming was getting on his nerves. He'd played around with enough kits to know there was a power current running through the lock, holding the bolt in place.

Wait a minute . . .

The current had to be on to make the lock work. If the current was disrupted or went off . . .

It would open.

He looked up through the ventilation hole. Three cables spiraled off the tray that served this room. One was lighting, the second was the alarm, and the third had to be security.

Break the security cable and the door lock would fail.

Heart pumping now and all pain forgotten, Dan hopped back up onto the door handle and hooked his fingers around the edge of the hole above him. He swung off and hung there, looking for the cable. His arms and shoulders ached already, and the rough edge cut into his fingers. He snatched the cable, the blue one, and pulled. It held.

He tightened his grip and let go of the ceiling.

His whole body weight behind him, the cable ripped free and he landed clumsily.

The humming died, and the door bolt clicked.

Dan got up, approached the door, and took hold of the handle.

Escape. Escape. Escape.

He turned it and swung the door open.

The corridor smelled of fresh paint and wasn't quite finished. There were spools of cables and pipes neatly piled along the wall for when the workmen returned to finish. Dan grabbed a length of pipe, a foot long and made of steel. It wasn't much of a weapon, but he felt better holding it.

Dan raced along the corridor, all senses alert. Barefoot, he made no noise at all.

He needed supplies. Clothing. Food. Boots.

He came up to a changing room. He listened before entering.

Steam filled the room from the running showers. He could hear the voices of a couple of guys chatting over the rush of the water. Lockers lined one side of the wall and there was a bench with clothes lying on it. Dan threw on a pair of jeans, measured his feet against a pair of sneakers, and found them a close enough fit. Then he threw a hoodie on, pulling the hood over his head. He was about to leave when he spotted a security tag hanging from the clothes hook. He grabbed it and strung it around his neck. Never mind that he looked nothing like Dr. Justin Klingerhoff.

Escape. Escape. Escape.

Which way next? He needed to find food, even if it was only a packet of breakfast cereal. His belly rumbled, reminding him it had been a long time since it had been filled.

Dan reached a door marked RESTRICTED ACCESS and tried his security tag. The door lock clicked and he went through. He was in business.

Dan stopped dead in his tracks. He gazed up and up and up.

Now he knew why it was called the Hive.

CHAPTER 42

Attleboro, Massachusetts

Vikram Kabra downed his fourth (or was it fifth?) glass of champagne. It tasted . . . bitter.

That's the flavor of your life, Kabra.

All around him was the mewling of cats. That's what the other guests sounded like. All fake joviality and pasted-on charm.

They were celebrating a bitter harvest.

What had any of them done? What had he done?

Joined forces with a traitor to claim what they thought they deserved.

He looked sourly at the gathered survivors of Nathaniel's purge of the Cahill family. Were they the beginnings of a new, golden era, or were they the few refugees, bobbing in a leaky life raft, watching their world disappear below the waves forever?

He could see the tension, the stiffness, and the wariness. They might be mewling like cats, but that didn't fool him. They were wolves.

He felt nothing but disgust, at them, at himself. For he knew he was no better. Just like them, he was waiting.

Nathaniel's done us a favor. Destroyed our rivals for us. All we need to do is wait him out. He's an old, old man, after all. Then, which of us will rule?

Vikram liked his chances. Plans were already in place. Gifts (okay, bribes) had been handed out to a few here, to guarantee support when the time came, though in a company led by a traitor he expected a few would double-cross him at some point. Which is where the blackmail came in. Everyone had dirty secrets and Vikram, using his Lucian cunning, had worked hard to uncover those secrets. He had interesting files on most in this greenhouse. A call to Interpol would remove three, and an e-mail would have the FBI paying an unexpected visit to two others.

All in good time, Kabra.

He glanced up at the mansion, where his son was now imprisoned.

His son—what a joke!

Vikram had tried. He'd been hard and pointed out where Ian had failed, all to make him better. Compassion, fairness, and loyalty were tools—no, were crutches—for the weak, and no Kabra should have such . . . failings. The ability to inspire fear, the hunger for power, and a taste for ruthlessness—these were the qualities a true leader should have, and Ian lacked each and every one of them.

Vikram laughed as he remembered the look his son had given that girl Cara. He loved her! How pathetic!

I love no one. That's what makes me strong. That's what makes me better.

But Vikram caught himself, bleary-eyed, reflected in the greenhouse glass. Even in this crowd, he felt alone. Totally alone.

Look at yourself. Look how pitiful you really are. You haven't built a single thing, only destroyed. What is your legacy, Kabra?

"No!" Vikram hurled his champagne flute at the reflection. The glass shattered.

"Are you all right, Kabra?" Magnus looked down at him, with just a hint of a sneer. "The celebration getting the better of you?"

"It's too hot in here." Vikram pressed the button controlling the ventilation panels. "Why won't they open?" He punched them. Nothing.

Magnus raised his hand as he looked around. "Shh. Something's happening."

The doors to the greenhouse closed. Their locks hummed shut. The laughter and the mewling stopped.

One entire wall of the greenhouse buzzed. It turned opaque and then began to glow.

"It's a video screen. Very neat," said one of the Ekats. He wiped his glasses for a better view.

It was hot in here. Hot and sticky. Bees buzzed through the air.

The wall screen brightened and Nathaniel came into view. He looked down at the gathering like some Olympian god. "Ah, my friends, all gathered together. Perfect. I am sorry I cannot be here personally to greet you." The smile widened. "And to say good-bye . . ."

CHAPTER 43

The Hive, Alaska

Great towering columns of amber rose in elegant, regimented rows, spreading in all directions. Bees drowsily drifted from large ceramic ponds, all precision-made with exact dimensions and being steadily pumped with syrupy fluid. It was cold in here, making the few still-active bees slow and drowsy.

And what bees. Nothing like Dan had ever seen.

Some were the size of his fist, with wings shimmering with radiant color.

It was truly a vast hive. The columns were artificial homes and the ponds filled with some sort of nectar substitute, keeping the bees fat and healthy.

Dan walked slowly between the columns, peering in. Each was packed with slumbering bees. Most lay asleep; a few clambered over the stacks, making their way into hexagonal apartments of Plexiglas and honeycomb.

The columns had to be thirty feet high at least,

and this was just on the ground level. The Hive itself was over a hundred feet tall, and there were additional platforms, likewise crowded with more artificial hives, some tall and narrow, others cuboids or suspended and polyhedral with twenty faces or more, allowing bees access from all directions.

How many bees were in here? A billion? More? And this was just one of the three geo-domes.

A bee settled down on the edge of a feeding platform. Dan leaned closer to look.

It wasn't the traditional yellow-and-black. Instead, the colors were more vividly golden, and the black the mark of a . . . skull. The wings settled, and they too were unlike any Dan had ever seen. The stinger would have terrified a scorpion.

These insects were lab-made. Genetically modified.

Of all the things he'd expected of the Outcast, beekeeper was way, way down on the list.

But was there a way out of here? Freedom was just on the other side of the Hive's glass wall. Snow was piled up against it a foot or two high. The trees beyond swayed and there were mountains. A million places to hide.

There were large vents at the top of the wall. With manual controls to open them. If he could climb up, then he could crawl through the vents and be out.

No good. The walls are too smooth. I need to find another way—

Dan heard voices. He hid.

Two scientists were adjusting the flow to one of the feeding platforms, and a small pond filled with a viscous amber fluid. One carried a Plexiglas box with more sleeping bees.

"I felt sorry for the kid," said scientist number one, a guy with a bright ginger beard. "Hartford pushed too hard. I'm surprised the kid made it."

"Those Cahills have a reputation," said the second, the one with the bees. "You won't believe some of the stories I've heard. Dan Cahill jumped from the edge of space. He's a tough one. Anyway, we got what we wanted, didn't we?"

Ginger nodded. "Still, I don't like it. Don't tell me you don't feel it, too. What are we doing?"

"Following Hartford's orders, that's what."

Ginger scowled and looked uneasily at the box. "You think you should let them out now? What if one of them stings me?"

"You related to any Cahills?"

Ginger shook his head.

"Then you've got nothing to worry about, do you?" He reached for the box and slid the side panel open. "Wake up, you beauties."

The bees stirred as the man shook the box. They rose into the air and settled onto the pond to feed.

The two scientists gazed at the bees. Ginger shook his head. "Say what you like, but Nathaniel Hartford

is a genius. Give it a few years and these bees will be all over the world."

"Building a better bee." The second man watched a bee buzzing around him. "And a perfect army."

The pair turned and left.

Dan stared at the bees.

A chill dread fell over him as one buzzed near him.

You related to any Cahills?

Dan backed away from the hovering insect.

Bees pollinated the vast majority of the world's crops. He'd read that many were dying out, thanks to pesticides and chemical treatments in the foliage.

That had to be what the scientist had meant. These bees were resistant to the contaminants.

So they would survive when the other bees couldn't, and they would *spread*.

He searched his memory, forcing it to replay that last meeting with Nathaniel.

What had the Outcast told him?

That he wanted the formula from Dan, not to make his own but to . . .

Corrupt it. To turn it into a poison.

One that would wipe out the Cahills forever.

Dan gazed about him, appalled at the scale of the plan, of the Outcast's obsession. So that was what Nathaniel meant by his army. He'd bred the biggest army in the world. It wasn't made up of hundreds of thousands, but *millions*.

The bee settled on a flower and began probing for nectar.

Nathaniel had created his poison and he'd somehow bound it to the bees.

Bees whose sting would kill Cahills.

CHAPTER 44

Doors at one end of the chamber hissed open.

Whoever it was moved cautiously. Guards? Maybe they'd seen his cell was empty and were searching for him.

He shouldn't hang around. Let this guy go past and sneak out.

Just sit quietly and do nothing. He won't see me here.

Then Dan saw who it was.

Alek Spasky.

He carried a submachine gun and was scanning left and right.

Dan trembled. The rage beat hard in his chest. This guy had murdered Amy.

All that he'd been through, he'd never felt such pure, consuming hate. He wanted to roar, scream out the anger seething through him.

But that would give Alek the shot.

Dan tightened his grip on the length of pipe.

There was someone else exploring, just as quietly and just as cautiously, but Dan didn't see or care.

He slid a few inches forward. The bush rustled, but the Russian didn't notice.

They were level, Dan hidden, Alek's grip firmly on his weapon.

I'll have one chance. One chance to take him out.

Wait. Wait.

His hands sweated badly, and he was gripping the steel pipe so hard his fingers ached.

Alek took a step past him and Dan moved. He moved slowly, one step carefully down before the next.

Tears threatened to blind him. He couldn't help thinking about Amy. She'd died at the hands of this psychopath, alone and without her brother. After all the dangers they'd faced together, it had ended like this.

Dan gritted his teeth.

Nothing would bring her back, but Alek would never hurt anyone ever again.

He raised his pipe.

It must have been his breath, or the rustle of his clothing, but Alek stiffened. He turned.

Their eyes met and Dan swung.

Alek tried to block the attack, but Dan's blow was filled with fury and caught Alek across the jaw. He fell and Dan hit him again, just to be sure.

The ex-assassin lay stunned, bleeding, on the floor.

Dan picked up Alek's submachine gun.

Alek groaned, his eyelids fluttering as he fought off unconsciousness. "Boy, you don't understand—"

Dan pushed the barrel into Alek's forehead. "Shut your mouth."

Dan rested his finger against the trigger. All it needed was a gentle squeeze.

Amy had been so scared, staring at him. She'd wanted to tell him something, he'd sensed it, but he had no time, no choice. She was gone now, and there'd been so much to say. He'd thought he'd have a lifetime to tell her.

Just a squeeze.

But his finger wouldn't move that fateful distance. Enough to activate the hammer that would strike the cartridge that would spark an explosion that would generate a sudden expansion of gas that, constrained within the narrow steel barrel, would force a projectile at high velocity the foot and a half through and end a person's life, extinguishing all he was, and would be.

All that, from just a mere squeeze.

What sort of man would he become if he pulled this trigger?

Would it be one Amy would have wanted him to be?

"Dan!"

He shook his head. He could hear her. It was as if she were right beside him.

"Dan!"

Dan bit his lip. She sounded so real. . . .

It was as if she was trying to tell him something.

"Please don't kill Alek. We need him."

Dan turned around, sure he was going insane.

Amy stood behind him, smiling. "Missed you, dweeb."

Dan dropped the gun and rushed into his sister's arms.

CHAPTER 45

The alarm went off before Amy could explain any-thing to Dan. That would have to wait. "Time to move," she said, taking her brother's hand.

They went to the door and hit the OPEN button.

Nothing happened.

She hit it again.

Nothing.

"I'm getting a really bad feeling about this." Dan peered around. "The bees are out."

"The bees?" asked Amy. "What about them?"

Dan tore off a large leaf frond and handed it to her to wave the bees away. "Nathaniel's dosed them with a poison. Their sting will kill us. Anyone with Cahill DNA."

"But there are millions in here. . . ."

The temperature within the Hive was going up. The bees were waking.

Clouds swarmed over the nectar pools. More and more buzzed around the artificial hives.

"You sure about this?" asked Amy.

"No one's *that* fond of honey," said Dan. "Their

sting is fatal to anyone with Cahill DNA. That was his plan all along."

Amy flicked out her cell. She had the whole team on group text. She knocked out a warning.

Nat's plan is killer bees. Stay away! They're deadly to Cahills!

Alek pushed forward and struck the door with the gun. The reinforced glass shook but didn't break—there wasn't even a scratch. "Stand back, I'm going to shoot."

A bee settled on Amy's arm. She screamed and shook it off. But as she stared behind her, she saw they were covering the flowers and other plants. The air buzzed, thick with the insects.

The lights in the observation balcony flickered, then brightened.

It wasn't empty anymore.

Nathaniel stood right up against the glass, smiling broadly. Three of his guards stood respectfully behind him.

Nathaniel tapped a microphone pinned to his collar.

Hidden speakers within the Hive crackled.

"I wouldn't waste your bullets," said Nathaniel. "The glass is quite invulnerable to mere gunfire."

Alek snarled and raised his submachine gun.

Bullets burst across the glass window of the observation deck. The sound was deafening as he fired a few bursts into it. Bullets ricocheted off, splintering a tree and splashing into the feeding ponds.

Nathaniel stood there, unmoved and safe. "Told you."

Alek tossed the gun away. "No harm in trying."

Sweat ran from Amy's brow and down her back. It had to be hitting a hundred.

Another bee landed on her, this time on her neck. She felt its legs creep across her bare skin. "Dan . . ."

"Don't move, sis." Dan carefully flicked it off.

Nathaniel leaned onto the glass, watching eagerly. "All it takes is a single sting."

CHAPTER 46

Attleboro, Massachusetts

"Stand back," said Cara. She lay down and bunched her knees up to her chin.

Then she snapped straight, putting both feet through the window.

Ian helped her up, and they leaned out for a better look.

"Something's going on in the greenhouse," he said. "Nathaniel's making his move."

"With the killer bees," said Cara. She'd just read Amy's text.

Cara tested the iron gutter running along this part of the roof. It creaked and she felt a few brackets give a little. "Whoa."

"What are you trying to do?"

Cara scanned the roof. "To get to that drainpipe and shinny down. Get them out of the greenhouse."

"Two things. First, that greenhouse is unbreakable. You'd need to drop a couple of tons on it to smash it. Two, the roof needs some maintenance.

That drainpipe will come straight out of the wall if you put any weight on it."

"Maintenance?" Cara asked. "Like what?"

Ian got defensive. "The last inhabitants, namely Amy and Dan Cahill, blew the maintenance budget on upgrading the computer system and on a satellite. I was planning to get the roof redone, but the contractor I wanted was still finishing an earlier job."

"I can't believe you couldn't pull some strings to jump the line on that."

"It was Buckingham Palace, Cara," said Ian.

"So what you're saying is, the roof's ready to collapse?"

"No, of course not. Just bits of it are . . . somewhat loose."

Cara's gaze fell on the chimney about twenty-five feet away. She had an idea. "What about that one?"

"As wobbly as jelly."

They were fifty feet up. The chimney itself was maybe ten feet high. The greenhouse was long, the front faced the pond, but the nearest side of it wasn't more than, say . . . fifteen feet from the mansion?

Cara stepped onto the gutter. "Please hold . . ."

Ian stretched out to grab her but she was just beyond his reach. "Cara! Come back here!"

She shuffled along, fingers hooked on the roof tiles. "You want me, you'd better come out and get me."

"This is not some game, Cara!"

Her hands were sweating, and Cara fought to stop herself from trembling, from thinking about what would happen if the gutter gave way. A couple of pigeons watched, perched safely on top of the chimney pots.

She heard screams from within the greenhouse.

Don't get distracted. Keep your mind on the job.

Foot by foot she shuffled along the roof. The chimney had seemed so much closer when she'd viewed it from the window. That, and the roof had seemed less steep and the distance to the ground much shorter. There were a few decorative shrubs lined up below, but they wouldn't do much to cushion her fall.

Then, far longer than she wanted, she reached the chimney. She scrabbled up and lay down on the sloping roof, eyes closed, trying to gather her breath. Now, that was something she never wanted to do again.

"Make room for me," said Ian.

Cara opened her eyes.

Ian was fumbling his way behind her.

"What are you doing?" she cried.

"You said—"

Cara reached out and grabbed Ian by the collar and hauled him up beside her. He collapsed down next to her.

"This is cozy," he said. "In fact, I just might stay here until it's all over and someone calls for a helicopter to collect me because I am not going back the way I came."

"You are an idiot, Ian Kabra."

Ian laughed, and tears ran down his face. He wiped them eventually. "Sorry about that. Upper lip is now stiff."

Cara gripped his hand. "We'll do this together."

"Don't we always?" Ian flushed red. "Sorry, that slipped out. What about the bees? If we break the greenhouse, we'll save the people but free the bees, too."

"And where are they going to go? To those six beehives at the edge of the lawn. Let them. One gallon of bug spray and they'll be history."

Ian smiled. "You really are always one step ahead, aren't you?"

Cara grinned as she lay next to him. "Feet against the chimney. We need to get rocking, so push, then release. Then again, but harder each time. On three?"

He tightened his hold. "On three."

CHAPTER 47

"What have you done to deserve all this?" continued Nathaniel's projection. "Nothing. You've relied on the success of your betters and yes, I mean those children you so despise, and think you deserve what they earned through nothing more than your names."

Vikram stared at the image, appalled. People were running for the doors, fighting and trampling one another to get out, but the doors wouldn't open. Someone tried to smash a pane with a table but only ended up with splinters in his hands.

Vikram picked up a fallen chair and sat down. He collected an abandoned sorbet and watched Nathaniel.

Nathaniel's face had to be fifteen feet high, and his voice boomed from speakers in all corners of the greenhouse. There was no escaping him. *Which was what he must have planned all along*, thought Vikram.

And what was it with all these bees? He swatted one away.

"We've used one another," said the projection. "To destroy the Cahills. To break each component part so it crumbled under its own weight, and your treachery. Oh, a traitor recognizes his own. What surprises me is that Grace didn't have you eliminated, but then, perhaps, she was not as ruthless as we all thought. In the end, she was a sentimental old woman, wanting to hold her family together, not realizing what a nest of vipers had grown up around her heart."

He's talking about me.

Vikram sat, mesmerized. Could he deny any of this? Ian had become head of the Cahills and that had enraged him more than any of the boy's failures.

"Ow!" A woman stumbled back into a flower bed. "A bee stung me!" She stared at her arm, at the red swelling. "It really hurts . . ." Then, like a puppet whose strings have been snipped, she collapsed into the geraniums. Yellow bile bubbled from her mouth as she jerked.

Nathaniel clapped. He was watching this through cameras. "Ah, so very good! Her fate is yours."

People screamed. They clawed at the door and beat their fists, frantically, helplessly, at the unbreakable glass.

Vikram collected a champagne bottle. It was a sin to leave a bottle half finished. "Tell me more, Nathaniel."

"I did not put in all this effort, these last years of

my life, merely to hand the Cahill organization to one of you. I'm sure you were all counting the days till death claimed me. I can imagine how you'd cry at the funeral, then devour one another like wolves, all in the hope to become the next leader. None of you deserve it. As I have destroyed the rest of the Cahills, I now destroy you. The last, corrupt branch of a withered, decaying old tree."

Vikram raised the bottle. "Couldn't have said it better myself." A bee settled on his hand. He stared at it. "Hello, Mr. Bumblebee. Have you come to kill me?"

He wondered what the honey would taste like, made from the dead.

Vikram gazed up at Nathaniel's image. "I suggest a toast . . ."

Hmm. What was that noise? It sounded like hailstones on the roof.

Nathaniel's smile became a gruesome, skull-like grin. "My work here is done. As a wise man once said, you can never trust a trait—"

Then the world around them shattered into glass, stone, and flowers.

CHAPTER 48

The Hive, Alaska

"Don't move," Alek warned, as more of the bees settled onto Amy, Dan, and the Russian, too. "If you don't agitate them, they won't sting you."

Amy fought the panic rising in her chest. Her breath was coming in rapid, panicky gasps.

Bees crawled over her. They crept over her arms, along her neck, her head; one even searched along the edge of her ear. There was another, prodding her lips.

Dan stood there, body stiff, as the bees covered him like a coat. He had his eyes closed and there was one on his eyelid. His hands were clenched into tense fists and he couldn't believe how controlled he was.

Amy itched everywhere; it was agony not to move.

With one eye, she peered at the deck above her.

Perfectly sealed from the Hive, Nathaniel stood there, watching, waiting for the moment they'd move, twitch, give in, and then be stung.

A bee found a gap in her collar and was trying to creep down her back.

Alek was as covered as they were.

It was getting hard to breathe; the heat was rising and rising. Amy was suffocating.

Heat. That was it. The heat was waking the bees up. "Wait. There is a way to kill the bees. Or force them back to sleep. We need to drop the temperature."

"We could let the snow in." Dan gestured, slowly, with his thumb. "There's a control to the windows. Can you see the outer wall?"

"Yes." She could see it and the snowy, wind-driven landscape beyond. There was a snowstorm blowing, not that she could feel it, trapped in this buzzing sauna. Amy turned her head ever so slowly. "There's a winch."

"The manual override," confirmed Alek. "It'll open up the windows and let the snow in. The bees will fall asleep and die."

"It's no good. You move and you'll get stung. You'll be dead in a minute."

"A minute you'd better use wisely." He smiled at her. "Good-bye, young Cahill."

"No!"

Alek swept the bees off his face and ran. The swarm around him reacted angrily. He slapped his bare hand but Amy saw the bright scarlet stings.

"Stop him!" roared Nathaniel.

The guards hesitated. No one wanted to enter the death trap.

Nathaniel glared at them. "I gave you an order!" He hit a control button and the door to the observation deck slid open. He thrust his cane at it. "Go and stop him!"

The window vents cracked open and icy wind blew in. Bees crowded above them, circling in a panic at the sudden cold.

"STOP HIM!" yelled Nathaniel, his voice booming through the speakers around them.

Alek cried out. Bee stings covered his bare face and hands, creating hideous swelling. He sank to the floor as the bees fled from the cold.

But the guards had other ideas. They dropped their weapons and fled.

Dan shook himself as the bees flew off him. Snow was drifting in as the windows widened. He brushed insects off Amy. "You clear?"

"There's one down the back of my shirt!"

"Where?" He turned her around. "Wait! I see something moving!"

"Then squash it!"

"What if it stings you?"

"Squash it, Dan!"

Dan slammed his palm against the middle of her back.

Amy stood, too terrified to move. Too terrified to breathe. Then she did. There was a yucky, sticky patch on her back, but no sting.

She ran to Alek.

He was still alive, but his breath pumped raggedly. His face was swollen, and yellow bile dripped from his mouth. His eyelids had puffed up so he was staring just through the slits. He was speaking, but she could barely hear him.

Alek took her hand. His grasp was weak and the skin feverishly hot.

"Alek . . ."

There was nothing she could do but listen to his last words. Amy leaned closer.

Alek licked his lips. "Natalia . . ."

It was his last word, spoken with his last breath.

The bees fled from the cold. The temperature in the Hive had plummeted within seconds and they sought warmth. They swarmed, searching to escape the chill. Already whole sections of the floor were covered in bees, either asleep or dead.

But there was one place here that remained protected against the chill.

The observation deck.

They crawled through the vents and small openings. The steel grilles were thick with bees as they gathered in dense crowds, seeking warmth.

Dan beat his fists against the door. "It's locked from the inside! Open the door, Nathaniel! Open the door!"

Amy stared. Bees covered everything. They were on the walls, the consoles, over the furniture and Nathaniel.

The deck was soundproof, and Amy was thankful. She could see him screaming, flailing wildly at the bees, trying to beat them off with his walking stick. It was hopeless.

"Open up!" Dan yelled.

Nathaniel's face was hideously transformed with furious red swellings. His hands had doubled in size and his eyes were thick with yellowish poison. Bile frothed at his mouth as he stumbled blindly, tripping over a chair. He fell, and the bees covered him. Amy stared as he tried to get up, but then he sank slowly, and moved no more.

Her grandfather and her enemy, Nathaniel Hartford, was dead.

CHAPTER 49

Attleboro, Massachusetts
A week later

What were you thinking, Grace?

Amy gazed up at the portrait of Grace Cahill.

Oil paint lay thick upon the canvas, less of a painting, more like a carving.

Grace's mouth was a firm, straight line and her eyes had been piled with blue and flicked with icy white. She was gazing somewhere. The sunlight caught half her face, the rest was hidden in the shadows.

The artist had known this was a woman with many secrets.

Amy adjusted it on the wall. The new frame was dark mahogany, and had been the only reason the portrait had survived the fire that had destroyed the Cahill mansion a few years back. It had been sent off to be fitted with a new frame. It must have been one of the last things Grace had done before her death. In the chaos that had followed, it had simply been forgotten.

Now it was back.

Amy felt as if she were meeting Grace all over again.

What had she been thinking during those long, still hours in her study? Amy could make a guess. The Cahills. Always the Cahills. This branch or that. Who would take over for her, how long she could last at the helm. Who her friends were, and which of her enemies she needed to destroy.

Once, Amy had wanted to grow up to be just like her grandmother.

Now, not so much.

She'd admired her fierce love, her determination and pride in what she was, and what she'd achieved.

But it had all come at a cost. The loss of those she loved, of cutting off from those who loved her, of being so terribly alone.

The artist had known that too when he'd painted those eyes. They were not eyes that wept.

What would you do now?

Dan entered the study. He stood there, a doughnut in his hand. "They're waiting."

"I know. I'm almost ready."

"You don't look it."

Amy winced. There was no hiding anything from him. "Is it that obvious?"

Dan walked over to look at the portrait. "The bad guys are beaten, our friends are here, and we're home. So what's wrong?"

"So much has changed, so much has happened, but I can't help feeling we're back where we started."

"Like Grace planned it this way?"

Dan was right. That's what was bugging Amy so much.

Grace had been such a big presence in their lives, one they'd needed, and yet—

"She can't let go, can she?" Amy said. "It's like she's still sitting at that desk, ordering everything around us."

"You need to take that painting down, then, and put it up in the attic. Better yet, give it to Ian."

Amy wasn't too sure she'd wish a watchful Grace on anyone. "I don't know what's wrong with me. I've been head of the family before." Amy stood at the window and gazed down at the lawn and the party that had spilled out from the library, where the meeting was meant to be held in, oh, exactly three minutes. "This should be easy."

"Except you know it isn't, right? That even after everything, running the Cahills may"—Dan hadn't moved from the portrait—"turn you into her."

"It cost her everything, didn't it?" said Amy. "Was that what she was thinking, in that portrait? *Is it worth all this?*"

"You can only answer for yourself, Amy." Dan waved his arm, the one with the watch on it. "Time's up, big sis."

* * *

There'd never been a Cahill gathering like it. Then again, the Cahills had never been so diminished.

There were a lot of people missing, a lot of important people.

Vikram—no surprise there. Amy reckoned they wouldn't see or hear much out of him for maybe the rest of their lives. If one thing had spoiled Ian's utter, ridiculous happiness, it was the lack of response from his father. The man was never going to change, but Ian was. He was looking forward, not back. He didn't need his family's approval anymore to be happy. He had Cara.

All those who'd sided with Nathaniel had abandoned the Cahills. Maybe they were worried about reprisals, that those they'd betrayed would come looking for revenge. Nathaniel had done his work well. He'd recruited the jealous, the envious, the bitter. Those who had grudges, big and small, against the Cahills. Those who couldn't accept that the young had a place at the table.

None of them were here.

Amy knew there were plenty here who would love nothing better than to smash down a few doors of the once high and mighty and, if she'd been more like Grace, she may have joined in.

But Grace's way was not hers, so she'd told the revenge-seekers there would be no retaliations. The right side had won, and that was better than any revenge.

Then there were the dead. There was a hollow

ache, not just in her, but in others, for those the Outcast had killed. The Lucians had lost more than the other branches, and Amy just needed a glance at the faces on the lawn to see how few Lucians there were.

She thought about Alek Spasky, now buried beside his beloved wife. He'd hunted them, put a gun to her head, and saved them.

Amy gazed out over the lawn. At her vast, weird, and magnificent family.

She had no idea who'd rented the bouncy castle but, somehow, it seemed right. What didn't seem right was Ham jumping around on it like a deranged kangaroo, despite the bandages. No amount of bullets could take the bounce out of a Tomas, it seemed.

Some Brit DJ, a close personal friend of Jonah's, was working the decks beside the pool, and it looked like this was going to be the first Cahill meeting where the dress code included bathing suits.

But the Cahills hadn't been *completely* handed over to the under-eighteens.

Fiske Cahill dominated the dance floor. It didn't matter what the DJ was playing, El Coyote had the moves for them all. He spun and kicked and clapped and wove dancers in and out, twirling Cara one minute, then whipping Nellie off her feet the next to spin her straight into the arms of the laughing Sammy.

"Ouch," said Dan as he saw Sammy stumble to the edge of the pool. "The boy's hurting."

"Mauled by a mutant bear and yet he still dances better than Ian."

The pair of them looked over at Ian doing . . . something. Stomping on imaginary ants?

"Yup" was all Dan could manage. He looked over at her. "Just relax."

"Thanks. Really helpful." Amy raised her hand. "If I could just say something—"

The DJ cranked up the volume. Ham double-flipped off the bouncy castle to roars from the crowd. Three Tomas chucked a pinstriped Lucian into the pool.

"Please, I just need to say—"

"EVERYONE SHUT UP!" yelled Dan. "BIG SIS WANTS A WORD!"

A wave of silence rolled out, starting with them and swiftly covering those who now were the Cahill family.

Ekats adjusted their glasses. The Lucians straightened their ties. The Tomas put down whatever heavy objects they were bench-pressing, and the Janus raised their cell phones to take shots, mainly selfies, but a few snapped Amy up on the patio, overlooking the lawn.

Amy flexed her fingers. This was it.

It wasn't what Grace would have wanted, she knew that, but it was what she wanted.

And it was what the Cahills needed.

She cleared her throat and smiled at Dan, beside her as always. Then she looked out at her family. "I know this has been a hard time, for all of us . . ."

CHAPTER 50

The party ended, like so many do, in the kitchen at some very late hour of the night. Or early hour of the morning.

Dan searched the chip bowl, licking his finger so he could collect the few broken crumbs settled on the bottom. "They still fishing people out of the pool?"

Ham joined him and took the bowl. "I'll show you how you do it." He tipped the bowl into his mouth. He handed it back. "There."

"Gee, thanks."

Ian and Cara loitered by the table. Dan could tell they were holding hands under it. Ian had loosened his tie and undone his top button. He hardly seemed the same person.

Nellie fussed over Sammy, who guarded his own chip bowl with the look of a pit bull whenever Ham strolled by.

Jonah waved his cell. "You have no idea how many times that clip of Ian dancing has been retweeted. I think you broke the Internet, bro."

Ian gave his wince-smile, that frozen look between injured pride and happiness. "I'm sorry? Did you say something?"

Amy came in. "That's the last of them. If the gardener finds any more in the morning, they'll need to make their own way home." She stopped and looked around. "Thanks for staying behind, guys. There's one thing left to discuss."

Ham groaned. Dan wasn't sure if it was because he didn't want to talk more business or he'd eaten too much and now his stomach had died.

Jonah put his cell away.

Amy perched herself on the side of the table. She'd kicked off, or lost, her shoes at one point and now swung her bare feet. "We agreed I should run the Cahills, didn't we?"

Murmurs of agreement. Why were they discussing this old news?

"And what happens when I turn into Grace?" she said. "And start building my own list of Outcasts? And what will we do when some of your names are on it?"

Dan stared at her. "That's never going to happen."

"Bro's right," said Jonah. "We're as tight a crew as ever." Ham gave him a fist bump.

"I bet that's exactly what Grace thought when she married Nathaniel. That nothing would get in the way of their love. Well, we know how wrong she was about that. One ruler of the Cahills is a recipe for disaster." Amy glanced at Dan. "The Romans had that problem, didn't they? What was the name they used?"

"Dictator," answered Dan. He might not have been an Ekat but he knew something about history. "Then, when the Republic collapsed, they called him 'emperor.'"

Cara frowned. It had to be serious, because she wasn't holding hands with Ian anymore. "So you're quitting again? Why didn't you say earlier?"

Amy smiled. "No, not quitting. I'll run the Cahills for a while. But only for a while."

"How long?" asked Ian.

Amy shrugged. "How does four years sound? Then I'll hand it over to one of you guys. After four years you hand it over to the next. Each branch gets its turn before it comes back to . . . someone new."

"Why?" Dan shifted forward. She hadn't said anything to him!

"Running the Cahills destroyed Grace, Dan. It's obvious. She stayed in it too long. In charge and all alone. You would think we'd be smarter than that but maybe that's the problem with smart people: They think they should *stay* in charge."

For some reason everyone looked at Ham. He put down his triple jelly-and-cucumber-and-mackerel sandwich. "What?"

Ian smiled and nodded slowly. "I like it. What shall we call it?"

Dan looked over at his big sis. He'd never been prouder of her, and of being a Cahill. "Democracy?"

SAIBNCEDAED
IASB
RAEBTCUDRENFIGNHG